A
Midnight
Clear

ALSO BY KATHERINE PATERSON

Angels and Other Strangers
Bridge to Terabithia
Come Sing, Jimmy Jo
Consider the Lilies (with John Paterson)
The Crane Wife (translator)
Flip-Flop Girl
The Great Gilly Hopkins
Jacob Have I Loved
The King's Equal
Lyddie
The Master Puppeteer
Of Nightingales That Weep
Park's Quest
Rebels of the Heavenly Kingdom
A Sense of Wonder (omnibus edition including Gates of
Exellence and The Spying Heart)
The Sign of the Chrysanthemum
The Smallest Cow in the World
The Tale of the Mandarin Ducks
The Tongue-cut Sparrow (translator)
Who Am I?

KATHERINE PATERSON

LODESTAR BOOKS

Dutton   New York

A

Midnight Clear

✸

STORIES FOR THE
CHRISTMAS SEASON

*No character in this book is intended to represent any actual person;
all the incidents of the stories are entirely fictional in nature.*

Library of Congress Cataloging-in-Publication Data
Paterson, Katherine.
A midnight clear : stories for the Christmas season /
Katherine Paterson.
p.   cm.
Contents: A midnight clear—Merit badges—Watchman, tell us of
the night—A stubborn sweetness—No room in the inn—Poor
little innocent lamb—In the desert, a highway—Star lady—
Amazing grace—Exultate jubilate—The handmaid of the Lord—My
name is Joseph.
ISBN 0-525-67529-9 (alk. paper)
1. Christmas—Juvenile fiction.   2. Children's stories, American.
[1. Christmas—Fiction.   2. Short stories.]   I. Title.
PZ7.P273Mi   1995
[Fic]—dc20   95-12590
CIP   AC

Published in the United States by Lodestar Books,
an affiliate of Dutton Children's Books,
a division of Penguin Books USA Inc.,
375 Hudson Street, New York, New York 10014

Published simultaneously in Canada by McClelland & Stewart, Toronto

Editor: Virginia Buckley
Printed in the U.S.A.   First Edition   10 9 8 7 6 5 4 3 2 1

for all the saints

of

Lafayette Presbyterian Church

Norfolk, Virginia

and

First Presbyterian Church

Barre, Vermont

with gratitude and love

Still through the cloven skies they come,
With peaceful wings unfurled;
And still their heavenly music floats
O'er all the weary world;
Above its sad and lowly plains
They bend on hovering wing:
And ever o'er its Babel sounds
The blessed angels sing.

"It Came Upon the Midnight Clear"
Edmund Hamilton Sears, 1810–1876

Contents

A Midnight Clear	1
Merit Badges	21
Watchman, Tell Us of the Night	42
A Stubborn Sweetness	53
No Room in the Inn	68
Poor Little Innocent Lamb	83
In the Desert, a Highway	102
Star Lady	127
Amazing Grace	148
Exultate Jubilate	163
The Handmaid of the Lord	178
My Name Is Joseph	194

A Midnight Clear

IN THE MIDDLE of the algebra test, Jeff saw the cloud for the first time. He couldn't make heads or tails of the fifth problem, so he did as he usually did when he was stuck: He looked out of the window. That was when he saw it—a huge mushroom cloud with an orange belly, oozing up from the new row houses across from the high school. He threw his hand in front of his eyes. His pencil bounced off the desk and clattered onto the floor.

"Pitman?" Mr. Channing asked. "You all right, Pitman?"

The cloud had disappeared. Behind the row houses there was nothing but a blue December sky. Jeff shook his head at the algebra teacher and leaned down for his pencil. The algebra test was a blur of blue lines and smudges. He picked the pencil up, gathered his books and notebooks from under the seat, and stumbled to the front of the room.

"You sick, Pitman?"

"Yeah, I think so. Like I'm gonna throw up or something." He didn't bother to ask Channing to let him finish the test later. He just handed it over and walked out of the school, back to the apartment. His mother would be furious. No, not furious. Before the divorce she got furious; now she got hurt or hysterical. He preferred furious, but then nobody was asking him.

The mail had come. He picked up *Newsweek* to read while he drank his milk. There was a picture of a mushroom cloud on the cover. His skin prickled all over, and he dropped the magazine to the floor. Not the milk. He was lucky it wasn't the milk.

At least that was a real picture of an atomic blast, not a hallucination. Because during the next few days, he saw, or thought he saw, the orange-bellied cloud three more times—once in English class and twice in nightmares.

Then school was out for the holidays. Several days before Christmas, Jeff went downtown, determined to do his shopping, although he didn't even want to think about Christmas. It brought back too many memories —like candlelight in church, and caroling, and huge, sweet-smelling trees—and the time when he was about three when his father took him to see the department-store Santa Claus.

Just as Jeff had gotten to the head of the line, the bearded guy had looked him straight in the eye and boomed out, "Ho! Ho! Ho!" Jeff had screamed for his daddy, and he had come running and picked Jeff up. And his daddy hadn't been embarrassed or anything. In fact, he'd fussed at the Santa for laughing so loud and scaring little kids. Jeff still remembered how his father had carried him all the way home.

"That wasn't the real Santa Claus," he had told Jeff. "Just a make-believe. A fake. Didn't even know how to laugh." And they'd both giggled at how stupid the old guy had been. . . . It had been a long time since the two of them had giggled together.

Jeff was going up the escalator, half-listening to the rinky-dink carols being played on the department store loudspeaker—they were as fake as that old Santa's laugh had been—when he saw the mushroom cloud again, right inside the department store, against the wall above the men's sweaters.

"Watch out! What do you think you're doing?"
But Jeff ignored the protests, pushing his way down the
up escalator as fast as he could and out the front door
of the store.

He was breathing hard and sweating despite the
cold. "Peace on the earth . . ." God, what a laugh. He
was almost crying.

He began walking out rapidly from the center of
town. How long before it will all be gone? he wondered. Exploding in the sky or smothered in freezing
darkness—either way it would all be gone. A stray dog
watched him coming and waited until Jeff drew alongside, lifting its nose and staring with sad brown eyes
into Jeff's face.

He knows, Jeff thought. Just a dumb mutt, and he
knows.

There were ropes of red and silver strung between
the light posts, and on each post a plastic candle in dirty
yellow.

What man would destroy, he first makes rinky-
dink. Jeff kicked a beer bottle someone had thrown
down. It skimmied across the pavement and crashed
against concrete steps.

"Hey, watch it!" The screech came from an old

woman who was sitting on the steps. "Ain't you got no respect?"

"I'm sorry." Jeff began to pick up the shattered brown glass.

"God's gonna get you, sonny." She jerked her head toward the building behind her. It was a large, graying stucco church. "God's gonna get you good."

"I really am sorry."

She must have been wearing four or five layers of clothes, and her head was wrapped in rags. He could even see the dingy lace of an ancient slip hanging out from under the tatters. Beside her on the steps were two large shopping bags. She reached into one of them and dug around, finally bringing out a large blue kerchief. She blew her nose noisily.

Then, suddenly, she began to cough—coughs that shook her whole body and seemed almost to shake the concrete step beneath her. Her face grew crimson, then almost blue, and she was choking, hardly able to breathe.

"Are you okay?" Jeff moved toward her, wondering what he should do. She shook him away.

Once more she reached into her bag and pulled out a bottle and a tablespoon that had lost most of its silverplate. Still coughing and gagging, she shakily poured some of the brown liquid into the spoon and jammed it into her mouth. It dribbled out the corners. She licked her lips and sent a long tongue down toward her whiskery chin.

"So? What are you staring at?"

"Nothing. I'm sorry." Jeff busied himself once more picking up the broken glass. He stood up, looking for a trash receptacle.

"Here," she said, holding out a sheet of newspaper.

"Thanks." He dropped the glass onto the paper, intending to throw it all away, but she drew back her hand and, folding the paper over the glass, put it into her shopping bag.

"Never know when it will come in handy," she said. "Ain't that right?"

"Sure," he said. "Sure."

"You think I'm crazy, don't you?"

"No, not at all."

"Liar."

For the first time in months, Jeff was beginning to enjoy himself. He had met a genuine original bag lady of the streets. "You're no crazier than me."

She cocked her head. "You don't look crazy—little stupid, maybe, not crazy."

"Oh, but you don't know. I—I see things." He had meant to joke, but in the middle, the familiar chill spurted through his body. Why had he said it?

"Yeah?" Her pale grayish eyes were glittering. "What do you see?" she asked.

He swallowed hard. Maybe if he told someone . . . "Clouds," he said, "mushroom clouds. Scares the devil out of me." He tried to smile, but his mouth stuck.

Something stirred behind the old eyes. "Like Japan? In the war?"

He nodded.

She sniffed, wiping her nose on a grubby rag. "Crazy not to be scared of that."

The chill passed. He liked the woman more every minute. "Mind if I sit down?"

"I don't. The reverend highness William P. Prisspot might." She pulled her shopping bags closer to make room for him.

"The reverend who?" he asked, wishing he'd thought to sit upwind of her.

"Aw, the preacher at this so-called church. He thinks I lower the property values or something, sitting on his fancy steps. God awmighty, at least I don't break beer bottles all over them."

"I said I was sorry."

"You don't want any supper, do you?"

"What? Oh, no, thanks," he said as she brought a white McDonald's sack from the shopping bag and took out what remained of a well-chewed hamburger.

"You'd be surprised what people throw away," she said, moving the hamburger around to where there were teeth to bite it.

"Mrs. Dodson!" The brown wooden door had opened behind them, and a man in a dark suit and blue tie was towering above them.

"Whoppedo," the old woman said through her burger. "It's neighborhood cleanup time."

The man came down the stairs and stood on the pavement in front of them, but he still seemed to be towering over them. "Mrs. Dodson, what are you doing here?"

Jeff was more surprised by the fact that the old woman had a name than by the fact that the minister knew it.

"I thought you were all settled into Friendship House."

"Oh, Preach, that place is worse than the slammer. I can't stay there. It's a bunch of eighty-year-old pick-pockets and streetwalkers. What's an honest old lady like me gonna do in a dump like that?"

"In the first place, Mrs. Dodson, you're about as honest as Jesse James. And in the second place, you're sick and have no business sleeping on the street in this weather."

"Well, it's your fault. If you'd let me sleep on one of them nice red-cushioned benches in there . . ."

"Mrs. Dodson, you know I can't let you do that."

"It's not as if you was crowded to the doors. You hardly got half a house Sunday morning, and you sure as Christmas don't have anybody there at night."

"It's a church, Mrs. Dodson, not a motel. Besides, it's not really up to me."

"Next you'll be telling me God won't let you."

"I'm afraid God doesn't have much to say about it. It's the church board that makes policies about the use of the building, and *they* feel you'd be much more comfortable in Friendship House."

"Well, Friendship House don't happen to suit me. I'm very sorry." She jabbed Jeff with her elbow. "That's your line, ain't it, sonny?" She put her palm on her chest and lifted her head. "I'm sorry, Reverend, so sorry, so very sorry." The old lady was an actress. He loved her.

"Would you introduce me to your young friend,

Mrs. Dodson?" the minister asked, interrupting her performance.

"What? Oh, the kid." She considered Jeff. "Just some crazy delinquent took up with me. Don't worry. I'll trash *him* before nighttime. The board wouldn't want him on their fancy benches."

"Does he have a name?" the minister asked, smiling at Jeff.

"Even a dog's got a name," she grumped. "I just don't happen to want to tell you. You'd ship him off to Friendship House to rot."

"Oh, come on, now, Mrs. Dodson. We're only trying to help."

"Yeah, that's what the snake said to Eve."

Jeff caught the minister's eye and they both started laughing. Jeff couldn't help himself. The woman was priceless.

"You see why I let this woman drive me crazy, don't you?" the man said.

Jeff nodded. Mrs. Dodson humphed and went back to chewing at her used hamburger.

"Mrs. Dodson," the minister said, "tell you what. You go back to Friendship House just for tonight. It's going to be freezing. Just go back there this one night, and by tomorrow I'll find you another place."

"Not the slammer."

"No."

"Not the state hospital."

He raised three fingers in a salute. "Scout's honor," he said.

She pretended to consider it. "How about five dollars for a nice warm supper? This hamburger's about wore out."

"You remember what you did with the five dollars I gave you last week?"

"Cough syrup. I got this terrible cough." She coughed a bit to prove it.

The minister pulled a wallet from his pocket. He took out a five-dollar bill. The woman reached for it, but he handed it to Jeff instead. "Would you do me a favor and take her down to the café at the corner of Fifth and Main and see that she gets some solid food in her? Now don't go pouting, Mrs. Dodson. You know what would happen to this money if I gave it to you."

She wouldn't let Jeff help carry the shopping bags. She insisted on dragging them herself the five blocks to the café. At least once on every block she fell into a fit of coughing, bending over with her rag-wrapped head nearly to the pavement.

At last he pushed open the café door and waited as she hauled herself and her possessions the last few feet into the warmth. "Hey, Rosie," someone yelled. "I see they let you out."

"Shut up," she replied pleasantly. She was obviously at ease here. "I got money," she said to the waitress, a woman of about sixty years with the build of a linebacker, "and I'll have the special." She turned to Jeff anxiously. "You hungry?"

"No," he said.

She smiled happily. "Too bad." She settled back. "A tall draft for me, Gert. And how 'bout"—she smiled mischievously—"how 'bout a side order of mushrooms for the boy?"

He flushed and began to fiddle with the edge of the paper napkin. The old woman leaned toward him. "Now don't let a little teasing curl your upper plate, sonny."

"It's okay," he said, not looking up. "The whole thing's pretty stupid. I know that."

"Be stupid not to be scared," she said.

He looked up. She was smiling at him. "You really think so?"

"Sure. You never know what those Japs'll do."

He almost started to explain to her that the Japanese had nothing to do with his fears, but it seemed too complicated, so he just smiled back.

The food came. It was all the same color—a thick white gravy covered the meat loaf and mashed potatoes, and there were white beans on the side. But she ate with enthusiasm. "Wanna bite?"

"No, thanks. My mom's expecting me."

"That's sweet," she said. "You having a mother. I figured you for a stray."

"Not quite," he said.

When she had finished, wiping the plate clean with a piece of white bread and lifting her empty glass three times to try to squeeze out another drop, she gave a big sigh and sagged back against the booth.

It was well past dusk outside. His mother would be hysterical. "How are you going to get to Friendship House?" he asked.

She looked up sharply. "It's only a couple blocks from here. I can walk her. No rush."

He hesitated.

"You better run along home. I want to just sit here for a while before committing myself to that fruit basket."

"You'll be all right?"

"Sonny, I been all right for seventy-eight years, which is more than I can say for you."

He paid Gert at the cash register. "I hope you didn't leave my tip on the table. Rosie will steal it, sure," Gert said as she took his money.

He flushed. He'd forgotten the tip, so he handed her the change. "It's from the church," he said.

"Yeah," she said. "I figured. What a bum."

"She's not a bum." Why on earth was he defending her? Of course she was a bum. But he hated the waitress for saying it. He borrowed a pencil and took a napkin off the counter and wrote his phone number on it. He walked back to the booth. "Here," he said, pulling a quarter from his pocket. "This is my phone number. In case you need somebody."

"You are crazy, ain't you?"

"Yep," he said. They both smiled.

HIS MOTHER WAS only slightly hysterical. He pretended to be offended by her so that he wouldn't have to talk during supper. He didn't want to have to explain that he was late because he had been taking a bag lady out to dinner.

He went to bed, thinking more about that crazy old woman than the end of the world. But once asleep, the nightmares returned. There was the blinding flash of light. He raised his arm to shield his face and he saw his own bones through the flesh. An alarm began to ring. He sat up sweating. It was the telephone.

He jumped out of bed, ran to the kitchen, and snatched it up. He was still panting.

"Sonny?"

"Who is this?"

"It's Rosie. Who's this?"

"It's me, Rosie. You woke me up."

"That's what you get for sleeping."

His mother was calling from her bedroom, asking who was on the phone. He covered the mouthpiece. "Just this girl I know, Mom. It's okay." She grumbled about telephone calls at ungodly hours, but he knew she liked the idea that some girl was calling him. Hoo-haw, what a girl.

"You still there, sonny?"

He cupped his hand around the receiver and spoke as quietly as he could. "Where are you? Are you all right?"

She began to cough in answer, choking and gasping.

"Rosie? Where are you?"

"I'm in the church," she managed to say. "It's cold as Hades in here. I think they turned off the stinking heat." She began to cough again. "I don't feel so great," she gasped out at last.

"I'm coming," he said.

"Side door," she managed to say before another spasm of coughing.

When he got to the side door of the church, it was open. He slipped in. Except for the red glow from the exit lights, it was pitch dark. He fumbled instinctively for a switch, but realized in time that more light was sure to bring the police.

"Rosie," he called softly, feeling his way down the corridor. "Rosie, where are you?" He heard her coughing and followed the sound. He could make out the dim outline of the pulpit to his left and the pews stretching back to his right. The smell of greenery spiced the cold air. "Rosie?"

She was slumped over in a pew near the front. He felt her forehead the way his mother used to feel his when he was small.

"I don't feel so good," she said.

"I think you have a fever," he said. "Shouldn't you go to a hospital?"

"Who do you think I am, sonny, Mrs. Nelson B. Vanderbilt?"

"If you go, they gotta take you in."

"We already figured out you was crazy, right?"

He sat down beside her. Her old face glowed red from the exit light over the side entrance.

"You see things, don't you, sonny?"

"Yeah."

"Can you see if I'm gonna die tonight or not?"

The idea of her dying was like looking at his own bones through his arm. "You're not going to die, Rosie."

"I'm gonna die. Maybe not tonight. But sometime soon enough."

"Don't say that."

"You care, don't you?" She twisted around to try to look at him. "That's kinda sweet." She settled back. "I like that."

They sat there in the silent darkness, her shoulder against his. Hers was wrapped in so many layers of clothing that there didn't seem to be a human body underneath, but there was. He knew there was.

"I'm scared, you know. I ain't been all that good. I figger God's gonna get me something awful."

He opened his mouth to reassure her when, suddenly, he saw it. A plain wooden cross hung from the beams over the pulpit, and right behind the cross, swelling up from the shadows at the back wall, the form of the terrible mushroom cloud. He punched her shoulder. "There, Rosie, you see it?"

She jerked her eyes open. "What? See what, sonny?"

"The cloud—there, right behind the cross."

"God awmighty. We're a pair." Then she hunched her shoulders and squinted. "That ain't no cloud, sonny. That's one of them fancy glass windows. Look again. That's angel's wings. See, there in the window. It's an angel."

And it was an angel—an angel bending over talking to a woman.

"Fear not." He said it out loud.

"What, sonny?"

"That's what the angel said, 'Fear not.' "

"That's sweet," she said. "I like it." She stretched out away from him on the bench, shoving his jacket with her tennis shoes so that he stood up. She sighed. "Maybe God ain't out to get me after all. Sent me my own private angel. Might be a crazy angel, but he's sweet." She punched the air in Jeff's direction so that he would know she was joking.

Jeff took off his jacket and put it over her legs, but it was hardly enough. He went back into the hall and nosed about until he found the choir room, which had a closet full of robes. He grabbed a handful from the rack and took them back to the sanctuary. He began covering her with the robes, but she seemed so quiet. What if she had died on him, here in this cold church? What could he do? "Rosie," he called softly. Then louder, "Rosie!"

She didn't move. All he had done was go to the choir room, and now she was dead.

"Rosie," he called hoarsely. "Are you all right?" Oh, God, don't let her die.

The old woman opened one eye. "Fear not," she said. "Fear not, sonny. Just get my bags from the ladies' room and get on home before your mother calls the cops."

He brought her bags. "Are you going to be okay?"

She snuggled under the mound of choir robes. "Sleeping in heavenly peace, sonny." She cackled. "Didn't know I knew that line, did you now?"

He patted her and took one last look at the angel over the altar. If he'd known how to pray properly, Jeff would have thanked someone. "Take care of her," he said to the angel or God or Jesus—whoever watched out for old bag ladies and crazy kids.

It was black outside, and bitter cold without his jacket. Above the darkened streets, the sky sagged under a load of stars. But there was one star, far more brilliant than the rest, its light almost touching the shadows of the houses—like a flaming solitary dancer low in the eastern sky.

Maybe he was seeing things again. Rosie was right. He was crazy. But this time he was not afraid.

A slightly different version of this story was published in The Big Book for Peace, *eds. Ann Durell and Marilyn Sachs. Dutton Children's Books, 1990.*

Merit Badges

"SCOUTS," Mrs. Bushey was saying, "we are entirely too involved in ourselves." It was all I could do to keep from snickering out loud. I didn't dare look at Amy. We'd both collapse. Mrs. Bushey always said "scouts," not "girls" or "kids" like a normal grown-up, or "students" like a teacher.

How did the woman ever get to be a scout leader, anyhow? I wondered. Well, of course, Judy quit to have a baby. That's how. They were desperate for somebody—anybody—to take over. But where would you dig up someone like Bushey? All of us called her Bushey behind her back. It absolutely fit. She had a bad home permanent that frizzed all over her strange little round head and she never shaved her legs. She was a sight.

"What?" I hadn't been paying attention. Apparently, Bushey had been plowing ahead with some harebrained scheme (no pun intended).

"Are we agreed then, Scout Hensen?"

"Sure, okay." What in the world had I agreed to do? I'd have to ask Amy afterward.

"Then here are the names of the residents and a little bit about each. We won't be able to make special friends with every one. We just wouldn't have the time, what with our busy school and activity schedules, would we?" Why did Bushey always say "we"? Didn't the woman know any other pronouns? *Residents?* I suddenly heard the word. What was Bushey talking about? What residents?

"There," said Bushey happily, "we have made a start in caring. We scouts must endeavor to be caring persons, mustn't we?"

The ten of us somehow got through Bushey's closing ceremony of the scout pledge and a song about friendship that must have been written about the time of the *Mayflower*.

We stumbled out of the dark church basement into

the late afternoon sunshine. But not before every other member of the troop was looking at me, their smirks exploding into shrieks. "Ah-ha, Kate, Bushwhacked, Bushwhacked." Amy had made up that term for anyone in the troop who let Bushey sucker her into something.

"What do you mean? I didn't get Bushwhacked. I wanted to."

"You're lying." Amy stared at me.

Now I was caught. I couldn't admit that I had no idea what I'd promised to do.

"Kate! You know perfectly well what happened when Judy took us there last Christmas."

"Christmas?" Here was a clue.

"The caroling. The 'disaster of the decade!'" That's what Judy had called our attempt to cheer up the residents at Logan Manor. My skin began to creep. Had I promised to do something at the manor? "That was just one crazy old woman," I said nervously.

"Sto—op!" Amy yelled. "Stop the noise!" imitating the old woman who had raced out of her room while we were singing "Silent Night." We'd been scared silly at the time, but now it was one of our group jokes. Whenever we wanted to make each other giggle, somebody would began imitating the old lady who had driven us out of the nursing home where we had gone to carol last Christmas.

All the others joined in. "Sto—op! Stop the noise!"

"So?" I pretended not to care. "She's not the only person there. I don't have to try to cheer *her* up. I can choose someone else."

"Aren't we a *good* scout?" Laura pinched her mouth in a perfect imitation of Bushey. "Shut up, Laura," I muttered. I could just see Bushey's frizzed head coming up the steps out of the basement.

It was bedtime before I looked at the list that Bushey had given me. It was typed, but obviously by someone who could barely do so. There were twenty-six names on the list. All women. All old. There were stars beside about ten of the names. At the bottom it said: "★These residents have no one who comes to visit on a regular basis." There were four names that had double stars. "★★These residents have no visitors."

Suddenly I felt freezing cold. I put on my bathrobe and went downstairs. My mother was still in the kitchen packing lunches for the next day. "Mom?"

"Katie. I thought you were already in bed."

"I'm just going."

She looked at me for a minute. "Is something the matter?"

"No." I felt silly and about four years old. "I guess—I guess I just wanted to come down and make sure you were here," I said.

She smiled. "Where else would I be, Pumpkin?" It was a baby name she hardly ever used anymore.

I kissed her cheek. "I love you, Mom."

"I love you, too. Now off to bed with you."

IT WAS A couple of days before I looked at the list again. By this time I'd decided several things. One, I would not choose anyone who *never* had visitors. That was likely to get me the stop-the-noise crazy one in that bunch. If I was going to do this—and none of my friends believed for a minute that I had the nerve—I would have to choose someone who wouldn't run me off or scare me to death.

On the other hand, it didn't seem quite fair to choose someone who already had regular visitors. That left the ten one-starred residents. The ones on this list with scary descriptions like "probable Alzheimer's" or "unable to speak" or "deaf" I crossed off. We were a scout, not a doctor or a psychologist, right? We were not going to bite off more than we could chew and give our friends the satisfaction of seeing us fail.

This got the list down to three residents. I chose Mildred Hull (husband deceased, no children, likes to play cards) because if you couldn't think of anything to say, you could always play cards. And besides, if the woman could play cards, she couldn't be totally off her rocker.

Monday afternoon was scout meeting. I was determined to make my first visit before then, but Sunday came and I still hadn't gone. I was tempted to ask Mom to go with me. But she and Dad had promised to do something at church. I dragged out my scout uniform, which had been in the closet since the "disaster of the decade." The sleeves cut me under the arms, and I looked really doofy. But I told myself it was like wearing a costume for Halloween. You could be someone else dressed up. I guess I needed the protection.

At the desk near the front door was a very skinny woman with an enormous head of hair that made her look lopsided. I bit the inside of my cheek to keep from giggling.

"Yes, honey?" the woman said. She didn't look like the kind of woman that would call you honey, but never mind. I cleared my throat. "I'm here to see Mrs. Hull," I said.

"Who?"

"Mrs. Mildred Hull." From barely a croak I went to a boom, and the woman ducked her head as if to say, "They're deaf, not me."

But all she said was: "Is Mildred expecting you?"

"Oh." I should have called. It was a little late to think of that now. "I don't think so. I'm Kathryn Hensen—I'm—from the Girl Scouts."

"Where is your leader?" That's what the aliens always want to know. I shrugged. Let her think my leader forgot or something.

She considered me. "Well," she said finally, "why don't you wait here while I go and see what Mildred's up to. A lot of our little people like to take a nap in the afternoon." Her voice dropped to a whisper as though she was letting me in on a big secret.

There was nothing to do but stand there by the desk while old women shuffled past, staring me up and down as if I was an endangered species in the zoo. The label of my uniform scratched the back of my neck, and I could feel the seams cutting the flesh under my arms. I should have worn something comfortable. But it was too late now.

Finally, the receptionist came trotting back. "This is Mildred," she said.

I was buffaloed. The receptionist was standing there all alone. For a minute I thought one of her "little people" was invisible, and then I realized that, clumping slowly up the long corridor behind a walker, was an old, old woman who must be Mildred Hull (husband deceased, no children).

I didn't know whether to run down the hall and stop the poor old thing from making the torturous trip all the way to the front desk or just to stand there and wait, trying not to stare.

"Mildred says she doesn't know you," said the receptionist as though to fill the time. "But some of our little people get confused."

Our little people? "No," I said. "No, she wouldn't have any way of knowing me."

"But wasn't your group here at Christmas, or was that some other—?"

"Uh, Mrs. Hull?" I double-stepped it down the hall toward the bent figure.

The white head twisted up, the arms leaning heavily on the metal frame. "Last time I checked," she said. "And you?"

"We—I'm Kate Hensen. I'm a Girl Scout." What were you supposed to say?

"Oh, I get it. I couldn't imagine why any young

girl I never heard of was coming to see me. I'm a merit badge."

"No. Really."

"Let me be a merit badge, please. I don't think I'm up to being a good deed for the day."

I guess I just stood there with my mouth open.

"If it's any comfort, our uniforms were worse. Lots worse." I tried to smile. "Well, if I can't get you a merit badge, what can I do for you?" she asked.

"Maybe we could sit down somewhere?"

"Sure. No stamina, you kids today. No stamina."

She clumped her way to the little sitting area near the front door. I followed her, my hands out ready to catch the woman if she stumbled. I hovered around while the she heaved herself into a straight chair and then nodded at me to take the overstuffed one next to it.

"Tell me about yourself," the old woman said, after she had caught her breath from the trip down the hall. "I haven't seen a live child close-up for ages. What are you like?"

"Like? Me?"

"Yeah. What would you be doing for example if you hadn't been shamed into coming to visit some poor little old lady today?"

"I— What?"

"Oh, come on now Kathryn or Kitty or—?"

"Kate. Everyone calls me Kate."

"Is that what you want to be called?"

"Well, yeah, I guess so."

"I like to call people what they want to be called." She lowered her voice and leaned toward me. "Stick, there," she whispered, jerking her head toward the receptionist, "calls me Mildred. I hate it."

"Stick?"

"Yeah, shhhh. We call her that because she looks like those stick figures little kids draw. You know."

I giggled out loud. I couldn't help myself.

"All these young aides here call me Mildred, too. I hate it. No one in my life ever called me Mildred."

"What do you want to be called?"

"My friends used to call me Millie." She leaned toward me again. "Promise you won't tell?"

I nodded, even though I had no idea what I was promising.

"My older brother used to call me Mildew."

"Mildew?" I looked at the woman, trying to see a little girl with a brother who called her Mildew. It was hard to imagine.

"For years, I burst into tears every time he said it," she said. "Silly, huh?"

"My brother used to call me Spook," I said.

"Spook?"

"My birthday is on Halloween. I hated that nickname. My mom calls me Pumpkin sometimes, and I don't mind at all."

"It's the way she says it, right?" She was quiet for a minute. "Ralph was my brother's friend. I was seventeen when I met him, and let me tell you the minute I saw that man I knew I wanted to marry him. When my brother introduced me as his sister, 'Mildew,' I was ready to kill him." She shook her head. "You know what Ralph called me till the day he died? Dewy." She gave her head a little shake. "Dewy. I thought it was the most beautiful name a girl could ever have."

I stared at her face hidden by thick, smudged glasses, trying hard to see that teenage girl so crazy with love. Then I realized Mrs. Hull was staring back and I said quickly, "Would you like to play some cards?"

"Cards? Why would I want to play cards? I hate cards."

"The, uh—" How could you tell a person they were on a list (husband deceased, no children)? "They—uh—told me you liked to play cards."

"I play cards. Sure. With people who can't make conversation. Why should I play with you?" She cocked her head. "I guess we scare kids, don't we, with our white heads and false teeth and all our handicaps and infirmities. Yeah, I guess that's it. We're like monsters, aren't we, to healthy children like you."

"No," I said, "really." But I felt a tingle as I said it.

"I thought we'd never see anyone under the age of fifty in here again after last Christmas."

"Last Christmas?"

"A bunch of kids—Girl Scouts, too. I remember the uniforms. They came in here all brave and shiny to give the poor old coots some holiday cheer—" She started to giggle. "You're not going to believe this—"

Try me.

"My roommate. She's a harmless old soul, but they woke her out of a sound sleep. And right in the middle of these little girls sweetly chirping away, she comes roaring out of the room screaming her head off. Those little green girls ran like Frankenstein himself was upon them." She started to laugh. "I'm sorry," she said, "it does seem mean to laugh, but it was the funniest sight we've had around here since Stick got her new hairdo. We'll never forget that night." She looked at me sharply. "You think we're cruel? Getting so much fun at the expense of those poor scared children?"

I shook my head. "Someday they will probably look back on it and laugh," I said.

"We take our fun where we can get it around here," she said, almost as if apologizing. "I really don't approve of making fun of people"—she jerked her head toward the receptionist—"with perhaps the one major exception. I used to say to my daughter, June, I'd say—"

Daughter?

"What's the matter? Oh. If I have a daughter, why am I here? Or why doesn't she come to see me? Is that it?"

"Well, they said—"

"She's dead."

What were you supposed to say to something like that? I opened my mouth, but there were no words.

"It was a long time ago. But it's hard, you know. No, of course you don't know. You're what? Ten? Eleven?"

"Almost twelve."

"I hope you never know. I thought when Ralph died I would never get over it, but losing your child —having your beautiful child die— Why should I be the one to live on and on?" she asked angrily. "What is my life worth? It isn't right," she said more quietly. "It's just not right." She fumbled around in the sleeve of the old housedress she was wearing. "Excuse me," she said. "This is embarrassing, but when I left my room, I didn't seem to bring a tissue."

I rooted in my pocket and pulled out a very wrinkled Kleenex. Mrs. Hull took off the thick glasses and wiped her eyes. "Thank you," she said. "You can mention that for the merit badge. Always be prepared. Or something like that. Don't tell them it was used. They may take off points."

"WE DON'T SUPPOSE we have anything to report about our project at Logan Manor?" Bushey looked wistful, like a kid asking Santa for a toy that she knew she wasn't going to get.

"I went Sunday afternoon," I said. The rest of the troop turned in their chairs to stare, but Bushey was smiling. She had a nice smile. She ought to smile more often.

"Yeah, I went through the list and picked a person they said didn't have any regular visitors. I didn't want to be running competition to somebody's darling grandchild."

"Did you get—you know who?" Laura whispered loudly.

"Who?" asked Bushey.

"This woman we met when we were caroling last year. No," I said to the others, "I was pretty careful about that." They laughed nervously.

"And?"

"Her name was Mrs. Hull and she said she didn't want to be my merit badge"—I ignored the noises the others were making—"but that she'd rather be a merit badge than a good deed."

"Which was she?" Amy asked.

"Neither. I liked her. I think she likes me, too. I'm going back to see her next week."

But Tuesday night Bushey called. The receptionist had made a mistake. Unaccompanied minors were not allowed to visit residents. "We could go with you," Bushey said.

"No!" As soon as I yelled it, I was sorry. "It's not you, Mrs. Bushey, it's the principle of the thing. I'm not going to misbehave. And I'm not going to give her some disease. I just want to talk with her. It wouldn't be the same with another person listening over our shoulders."

"If you're not comfortable with us, your mother might—"

"No, Mrs. Bushey, it's not you, really. I don't want my mother, either. I don't want to have to be baby-sat when I'm visiting with a friend."

"We understand," Bushey said, "and we think you're absolutely right. We will call the owner."

"Thanks, Bushey," I said, not even realizing that I'd forgotten the "Mrs.," "but I think Mrs. Hull and I can handle this."

"May we say how proud we are, Scout Hensen?"

"Sure," I said.

I called Logan Manor immediately, but the night person told me that it was too late for calls. "It's only eight," I said.

"Our little people need their rest." Apparently the night person was a Stick clone.

The next afternoon, they let me talk to Mrs. Hull who was, as I was sure she would be, outraged.

"You come over here and we'll give that Mervin Wertz a piece of your mind. At my age, I don't have any to spare. And don't wear your uniform. Wear something that fits and makes you look like your parents could buy this place out and have money left over to burn."

When I arrived, dressed in the suit that my grandmother had sent me for Easter, Stick was on duty. I even wore my only pair of panty hose. I had started to sneak some of Mom's makeup, but I was afraid she'd make a fuss.

"Oh yes, Kathy, isn't it?" Stick was rigid (pun intended).

"Kate Hensen. I think Mrs. Hull made an appointment for the two of us to speak to Mr. Wertz."

"Mildred and Gracie are already in his office," she said.

I opened the door. A man, a shriveled little man, was seated behind an enormous desk. Standing in front of him was Mrs. Hull, leaning on her walker with one hand and pounding on it with the other. In a chair on the opposite side of the room sat the person who Stick called Gracie, better known to me as "Stop-the-Noise." My blood froze, but I went into the room.

Mrs. Hull was saying something that ended with ". . . the Constitution of the United States of America."

Mr. Wertz was getting very small and very pale. Everyone turned to look at me. I was glad I'd dressed so carefully.

"Is this the child?" Mr. Wertz asked.

"She has a name!" Mrs. Hull shouted. "She has a name. She is a person!"

"Kate Hensen," I said. "How do you do, Mr. Wertz?" I walked over and offered him my hand. I was so polite and mature my grandmother would have fainted with joy.

Mr. Wertz ignored my hand. "It's very sweet of you little girls to want to cheer up our residents" (at least he didn't say "little people"), "but this is a medical and nursing facility, not a day care center." He smiled. I guess he thought it was a little joke. "We have some residents"—he gave Gracie a nervous glance—"who may be upset by unsupervised young visitors. And well, sometimes children are upset by elderly residents who, well, how shall I put it—?"

"Shut up!" Stop-the-Noise had jumped to her feet.

"As you see—"

"Shut up, I said!"

Mr. Wertz blinked rapidly. "Well, I don't really feel that we need to discuss this further. Our Gracie—"

"I'm not your Gracie!"

Mr. Wertz must have rung a bell or something because a young woman in a white uniform was there almost immediately. She took Gracie, or whatever Mrs. Hull's roommate was really named, by the arm and led her out of the room, shutting the door behind them. I could hear the old woman shouting down the hall as she went.

"You see, my dear, little children"—again my grandmother would have been proud that I didn't correct him—"sometimes, without even meaning to, can have an upsetting effect."

"Mr. Wertz, excuse me, but I think she was upset by you, not by me."

"She's right," Mrs. Hull said. "Mrs. Ticknor hates being called Gracie."

"We always call our people by their first names," Mr. Wertz said.

"I know," said Mrs. Hull, "and some of us always hate it."

I left that one alone. "Mr. Wertz," I said, "Mrs. Hull and I are friends—not close friends, I admit. We haven't had time for that. But we'd like to get to know each other better. We can't do that with chaperons. Frankly, we find the idea insulting. We are both perfectly intelligent people. I promise you that if you will allow me to come and visit Mrs. Hull, you will not regret it." I tried to put into my voice a hint that my family had untold millions, some of which would surely be donated to his nursing home if he agreed, but I can't be sure all that came through.

"And if it's any comfort to you, Mr. Wertz," said Mrs. Hull, "I will try to behave just as beautifully as my friend here."

"Whew," she said as we escaped after our triumph to a private corner of the lounge. "That was a near thing."

"Yeah," I said. "What's-her-name, Gracie, I mean—"

"Mrs. Ticknor to you," Mrs. Hull said. "Yeah, great, wasn't she?"

"What?"

"Yeah, right on cue. We couldn't have done it without her. Remind me to pick up a Hershey bar for her. Kind of our merit badge system. You know how it goes."

"I'm learning," I said.

BUSHEY AND I dragged the whole troop over to Logan Manor at Christmastime. Not to carol. Mrs. Hull vetoed that. We had a sing with the residents. Bushey, to my amazement, plays a mean piano, and Stick, when she unbends a bit, has a nice alto voice. Stick and I passed out songbooks, and the Girl Scouts scattered among the crowd. Gracie, I mean Mrs. Ticknor, mostly listened quietly, but when we got to "Joy to the World," I could hear her off-key "repeat the sounding joy" over and over long after the rest of us had gone on to the third verse. I smiled at Mrs. Hull, who smiled at me, and then Stick, who smiled at both of us. We all smiled at Bushey, who had a smile as wide as the stripes on the flag. We were all joyful. I think it was the first time I really understood the meaning of the word.

Watchman, Tell Us of the Night

I VOLUNTEERED TO work Christmas Eve because I was trying to put off going home. I mean, who wants to go home empty-handed at Christmastime? My wife would understand. She wasn't expecting anything. Fact was, she'd have been upset if I'd spent money for anything but food. Ever heard of a hungry farmer?

Well, okay, I'm not a farmer, not anymore. My father was, and his father before him. They left me their land and their dreams, and I lost it all. If only I hadn't bought the fancy new tractor, if only it had rained, if only I had planted soy instead of wheat, if only . . .

A bunch of if onlys and my house and land—my granddaddy's house and land—are auctioned off for a quarter of what they're worth. My wife and two little girls are in a run-down city walk-up. Sheila's six and Michelle is only four. I think what hurts as much as anything is that in a few years they won't even remember the farm—the green and gold of the fields, the old splintery wood barn that smells so sweet with hay, the baaing of the sheep and the jangling of their bells as they come back to the fold at sunset.

But, hey, I'm lucky—I got a job. Night watchman at Friedman's department store at the Pine Crest mall. I got me a blue uniform and a cap like a navy officer; a big flashlight, size of a baseball bat, on my belt; and this big holster with a pistol snug in the genuine leather. Lord forbid I ever have to use it. Like my daddy said, I couldn't hit the side of a barn with a M-16. He gave up taking me deer hunting by the time I was fifteen. I was hopeless, he said. Couldn't do nothing right. I'd probably end up shooting the game warden or something.

My Sheila, when she saw me all dressed up in my uniform, she told me I look just like a movie star. My wife bust out crying. I'm just glad my mother never lived to see this day. Or my dad. He'd never forgive me for losing his land. He hardly forgave me for being his kid in the first place.

But, hey, that's not the story I'm going to tell you. It's coming up Christmas, see, and nobody wants to work Christmas Eve. So the boss offers overtime for a six-to-six shift. I jump at it. I ain't got nothing but candy and two dollar-ninety-nine-cent stuffed bears to put in the kids' stockings anyway. If I work hard, maybe next year—who knows?

They close the store at six o'clock on Christmas Eve. By eight, when I look out the front door, the parking lot's almost empty, 'cept way to the north end where the all-night Peoples is sucking in a bunch of last-minute shoppers. I get so lonesome seeing all that empty asphalt, I just go back to the lounge, pour myself a cup of coffee, and turn on the radio. They're playing Christmas music. I nearly flip the dial. I mean, I'm not big on Christmas this year. But it isn't "Santa Claus is coming to town" they're playing. It's mostly carols. Hey, I tell myself, that's what Christmas is all about— Jesus being born in a barn—and it wasn't one that belonged to his daddy, either.

I don't want you to think I blame God or anything. Heck. It was probably all my fault. If I'd been smarter . . . My dad always said I was too dumb to milk a cow with both hands at the same time. But to tell you the truth, I'm not too big on God this year, either. I prayed. I really prayed. I couldn't believe God meant for me to lose that land. It was kind of a trust from my granddaddy, and he was a real fine Christian. He went to church three times a week and made his kids swear never to smoke or drink. My daddy never did, either. He was a deacon. When he died, there was standing room only in the church.

I used to go to that same church. Not every Sunday. Not easy for a farmer to get away every week. But my wife always went—took the kids to Sunday school and everything. When things started getting real tight, she told me I should pray more. So I tried. I really did. First I prayed it would rain. It didn't. Not hardly for two years. Then I prayed the John Deere guy would buy back the tractor for at least half of what I'd paid. He wouldn't. Then I prayed the price of wheat would go up. It fell out the bottom. Finally, I gave up praying for piddling little things. Hey, I said, forget the little stuff, just gimme a doggoned miracle.

So here I am. I've made my hourly rounds and it's about three o'clock in the morning. I'm listening to "While Shepherds Watched Their Flocks by Night" and thinking about how the first thing I had to sell off was my sheep. I loved those stupid sheep. My daddy wouldn't ever keep sheep. Too dumb for him. But maybe I wanted something around that made me feel smart. I'd look in the face of some old ewe, and she'd give me this worshiping look like she'd trust me with her whole silly life. I guess it's why some people keep dogs. Me, I like sheep. Yeah, I'd go for a miracle— one that would give me back enough land to keep a few sheep. How 'bout it, God?

There I was leaning back, my feet up on the table where the coffeemaker sits, my eyes closed, when I hear this noise. Or think I do. I slam my legs down, barely missing Mr. Coffee, and shut off the radio at the same time. And I just listen. There're a lot a noises in a big empty store at night, the heating system for one. The first night I was on duty I might have shot a heating duct in the heart if I hadn't caught myself in time —and if I had been able to shoot straight. My hand was shaking like a aspen in a gale wind.

Well, I sit there and listen to the heat go on and off—*ping*—and carry on. The wind is blowing the flaps of the vent in the ladies' room, and there's a couple of other squawks and groans that I'd never located but what I know by now are just part of the scenery. I don't hear them ordinary sounds anymore. I just hear the sound of my own breathing, which is hard and fast.

Then, I hear it again. It's faint and far away—must

be at the back of the building. Weird sound. Only thing I can figure it sounds like is some lamb out on the hillside bawling for its momma.

I shake my head to make sure it ain't cobwebbed and start out in the direction of the noise. There's lights on in the store, but they're low and kinda spooky. I'm sweating some. *Pull your gun. Don't walk toward any strange sound with your gun in the holster. You won't have time later.* Those were my instructions during my training. Training. Hah. Less than half a day. Then a couple of nights with another guard and I'm on my own.

I pull the gun out. I can still hear the sound. It's coming from the loading area, where crates are piled. Anybody could hide, drill me through the ticker, and I'd never know what hit me. I'm sweating so much now I have to stop, take off my hat, and wipe my face so I can see to walk through the door to the loading area.

Probably a cat. There're plenty of them behind the A & P, digging in the garbage. All we got behind Friedman's is empty cartons from the floor models, but how's a cat to know? A new cat on the block would have to nose around a bit, wouldn't he, 'fore he could find the garbage with the goodies?

I push the door out gentle and then sneak through,

gun in one hand, flashlight in the other, and *boom!* I'm sprawled on the dock. My flashlight goes one way and the stupid gun the other. It don't go off. I forgot to release the safety.

Anyhow, I yell, "Who's there?" and this box under my legs starts to squawl. Well, I figure whatever's in there ain't gonna shoot me, unless it's some delinquent midget, but I can't hardly stop shaking. Finally, I get up, get my flashlight and gun, put the gun back in the holster, and shine the light into this Zenith AM-FM stereo carton—right into the pinched-up bright red face of this baby. Yeah, baby. I mean little baby—hardly more'n a month or two old from the size.

"Hey, you!" I yell at the refrigerator cartons. "You come back here and get this kid!" The refrigerator cartons don't answer. Or the stove boxes or the dishwasher crates, either. "I mean it!" I yell, shining the beam all around. "You can't just walk off and leave your kid like this. It's against the law!" I wasn't sure about that, but if it ain't against the law, it oughtta be, right?

I keep yelling and watching for some sign of life rustling through the boxes, but it's still as the cover of the moon. Except for this kid, who by this time is squawling and shaking the box so hard that the *Zenith* looks like real lightning. I give up and take the box inside. It's cold as Hades on the loading dock. Shouldn't leave a baby out there. Shouldn't leave a baby at all.

On TV, when somebody leaves a kid on the door-step, there's always a note. Well, poking around the box, I don't come up with a note, but I do find a bottle, less than half full, plus one extra diaper. Not what you'd call long-range planning, but enough, maybe, to get me through till six.

First, I change the kid, and it's a boy. I never fussed about not having a boy. My girls are the sweetest little things you ever saw. I'm kind of a hero to them. And, well, I remember—my daddy and his daddy, my daddy and me. Maybe the men in my family don't do so good with sons. But here was this little guy churning his legs like a fullback and yelling his ugly little head off. I could feel something in my throat the size of a baseball.

The bottle is icy cold, as you could guess. I take off the nipple and warm the milk for a few seconds in the microwave. Then I test it on my wrist. Hey, you think I don't know how to do this stuff? I'm a pro. Two kids of my own and a small army of bottle-fed lambs, if you add them up over the years.

Okay, so you're wondering why I don't call the

cops. I could give you lots of reasons, but none of 'um would be true. I don't call the cops because it never once occurs to me. I guess something was niggling at me. Else why do I smuggle the kid in a shopping bag past Gus when he comes to relieve me at six? It's my secret. I don't want to have to explain it to Gus.

I get home. Usually I'm dog tired climbing those four flights to the apartment. This morning I just bounce up, baby and all. There're no lights on when I open the door. When I was a kid we used to get up in the middle of the night to see what Santa brought. I guess it's different for my girls. They've learned not to expect much.

We still got cloth diapers from when Michelle was a baby. I change the kid and wrap it in an old baby blanket and tiptoe into the bedroom, where I put it down on the bed beside Pauline.

"What time is it?" Pauline always wants to know the time. I kid her. The Day of Judgment, the trumpet will be blowing and Pauline will be asking Gabriel, "What time is it?"

"Merry Christmas," I say. "Look what I brought you."

Then she turns and sees the baby and her eyes get wide as satellite dishes. "What in the . . . ?"

"I was praying for a miracle," I say, "and here comes this baby."

She makes me explain, so I do, and then she says, "Why didn't you call the police?"

I don't want to tell her I never thought about it until that minute, so I say, "Why? The kid ain't done nothing wrong."

"You know what I mean." Pauline is the type that's very practical. And then, real soft, 'cause she's cuddling him and looking into his little pinched face: "We can't feed another kid, Gary. You know that."

I'm starting to try to figure out an answer, but the girls come running in. They see Pauline holding the baby, and Michelle is ready to explode she's so excited. "Baby Jesus! Baby Jesus! Sheila, Sheila, look! I told you Santa Claus was going to bring us something special!" Michelle hasn't got her various Christmas stories sorted out too good yet.

I look at Pauline and Pauline looks at me. Neither of us is gonna tell Michelle that somebody left this beautiful little ugly kid in a Zenith AM-FM stereo carton behind Friedman's department store.

This is our private little miracle, isn't it? Oh, I'll run a personal in the paper and ask the party that left a package on the loading dock at Friedman's to call the party below to identify contents and claim, but that's the most I'm gonna do for now. I'll figure out how to feed him—how to make him legal. Maybe I'll even figure out how to be a better father to him than my dad was to me.

But all that will wait for another day. I go down the four flights of stairs and out into the empty street. I want to watch the sun come up in the sky on Christmas morning, and I feel—how can I say it? I feel close to what it's all about for the first time in my life. Like I told Pauline, I prayed for a miracle, and God gave me a baby. Isn't that what He did that other time? Isn't that what all the cheering has been about all these years?

A Stubborn Sweetness

THE CALL CAME early Christmas Eve morning. I was still asleep, and my voice must have sounded peevish when I answered the phone.

"You needn't be annoyed with me, Judson," my sister said. "I can't help it."

"What is it, Fran?"

"What do you think it is? Why else would I call you at this hour?"

"Father?"

"Of course it's Father," she said. "The doctor is sure he won't last another day. He thinks you should come immediately."

Part of me wanted to protest. I didn't want to leave

my wife and children at Christmastime. What did it matter if I came or not? My father had not recognized me for ages. I dutifully went to see him three or four times a year. He would sit in his chair in the sterile nursing home, nodding at me. Sometimes, when he was most alert, he would call me Wesley. Wesley was my brother, who died in Vietnam. But usually he would mumble things I could not understand and nod uncomprehendingly as I would vainly try to carry on a conversation.

Once he looked me straight in the face, his eyes clearing, so that I thought for a moment he knew me, and perhaps he did, for what he said was: "Tell your mother Wesley's home." This time I nodded stupidly, not even trying to remind him that both Mother and Wesley had been dead for many years.

Part of me did not want to go and say good-bye to an old man who could not hear me, who had hardly listened to me even when we were both younger. And yet, I had to go. My wife understood, even though the children did not. "You need to go, Judson," Marilyn said, "not just for Fran's sake—for your own."

I drove myself to the airport, bought a standby ticket, and watched three flights take off without me. Each time, I called Fran to ask how he was. "You've got to hurry!" she'd say. But it was late afternoon before I got a plane headed for Springfield. When we landed, I called Marilyn. But when I tried to reach Fran, the line was busy, so rather than waste time, I rented a car and started the fifty-mile drive. The road on which I was traveling was new, but the countryside was the farmland in which I had grown up. The sky on this Christmas Eve was clear and star-filled, spreading peace over the rolling hills and the shadow of the mountain beyond. The world of regrets and sorrow and imminent death seemed far away.

I thought about my father—not the invalid he had become, but as I had known him when I was a boy. He was a strong, gruff man, a farmer who owed no man anything. If Wesley had lived, I think I might have grown up without my father ever really noticing me. Perhaps I'm unjust. I'm sure my mother would say so. She was forever trying to interpret us to each other, and for her sake, as we both grew older, we tried to understand. It was she on that terrible Christmas after Wesley's death . . .

Just then, my headlights caught a figure stepping out into the road. I swerved and missed, but I was shaken and, as I straightened the car, my heart still pounding, I caught a glimpse in the rearview mirror of the person I had nearly struck. He was in the road, waving his arms at me.

Without thinking, I stopped the car and began to back slowly down the shoulder. When I got alongside, I stuck my head out the window and shouted, "Get off the road! I nearly hit you!" It wasn't a man. It was a young girl, her hair streaming across a rucksack on her back. She wore no hat or gloves.

"Yeah?" Her chin was up. "Watch where you're going." Then suddenly, almost coy, "Hey, gimme a ride to town?" Without waiting for me to answer, she reached behind me, unlatched the back door, and was in the car before I could protest.

As I shifted into drive and moved out into the road, she swung the pack off her back and put it on the seat beside her. I had seen enough of her face now to realize that she was about the age of my daughter Jennie, who was barely fourteen.

"Where are you headed?" I asked, trying to sound casual.

"Who needs to know?"

"No one. I couldn't help wondering. You remind me of my daughter."

"Well, I ain't. Lucky you."

We drove on in silence. She was wrestling something from her rucksack. I switched on the radio. The car was filled with the joyful sound of a carol. My mind went from the waif behind me to my mother. She had loved Christmas so, especially the music. It was then that I felt the hard, round pressure against my right shoulder.

"Shut that thing off," she ordered.

I turned off the radio, too amazed to be truly frightened. Where on earth had the child gotten a gun?

"Now pass me back your wallet and watch. Anything valuable."

"I'll have to stop the car first."

"Okay, but no fooling around, hear?"

I eased the car onto the shoulder and shut off the engine. She held the gun, pointing roughly at my right ear while I got out of the car, took off my watch and wedding ring, and unloaded the pockets of my overcoat and trousers. I put the contents onto the passenger seat. Her hand was shaking as the gun followed my every move. I wasn't afraid she would shoot deliberately, but in her anxiety, she might accidentally—and then as I straightened up to close the door, I looked more closely at the trembling weapon. The car's dim overhead light gave away its secret. The gun was a toy.

My impulse was to grab it, laughing, but the look

on her face stopped me. Instead, I shut the door and began walking down the road.

She yelled after me. "Where the hell you think you're going?"

"I thought you wanted the car as well."

"Come back here," she said, her voice breaking. "I can't drive."

I came back and got in. The gun was at my shoulder at once. "Now go," she said, "and don't try to make a fool outta me again." She wasn't crying, but she was close to it.

"Don't use the credit cards."

"Shut up and drive."

"Seriously, they'll get you right away. There's about two hundred in cash, and day after tomorrow, you should be able to pawn the watch for at least a hundred. It's antique gold."

"What's with you?"

"I'm trying to help. I ran away from home once. It's no fun."

"I don't need help."

"Well, you do need money. You can't get far without that."

"Don't I know," she mumbled. After a minute, she

poked me hard with the plastic gun barrel. "You on the level about the credit cards?" she asked.

"I swear they're not worth it. I'd have to report them stolen."

"What about the watch and stuff?"

"If you'll let me have my wedding ring and the credit cards, you can take the money and the watch, and I'll consider them a Christmas present."

"Meaning?"

"I won't even call the police."

"Mister Santa Claus himself." Her voice was sarcastic, but the pressure on my shoulder lessened for a moment, and then she jabbed me hard. "You putting me on. I could kill you, you know."

"But it wouldn't be smart," I said. "And you don't strike me as a dumb person."

She snorted. "That isn't what my dad said. And he should know."

"Fathers aren't always right. My father . . ."

"Forget your father."

"I can't forget my father," I said. "He's dying. That's where I'm going. To see him once more before he dies."

"Dying?"

"It's all right. He's very old and sick. He's ready to die."

"Ask him. You might get another opinion."

"You think so?"

"I don't want to talk about it."

"Well, you're young . . ."

"But I might die," she blurted out. "Oh, God, I might die." The gun fell from my shoulder to the floor as she put both her hands to her face and began to cry.

"You dropped your gun," I said quietly.

She stopped crying instantly, snatched up the gun, poked me three or four times, then dropped it again. "You knew it was fake all the time, didn't you?"

I nodded.

"My dad is right. I'm the dumbest bitch in the world."

"You're not so dumb."

"Yeah? Then how come I'm pregnant?" She was almost yelling.

"Is that why you ran away?"

"It was either that or get throwed out. He don't care if I live or die. Long as I don't bother him."

My first thought was to rush in with words of reassurance. Of course her father cared. Even now he must be calling the state police, asking them to help him find her. But I kept quiet. I knew I was thinking of my father—what he would have done. I didn't know this child's father. And suddenly, I wanted to give her my father—for all his sternness and anger and doubts—because I knew what my father would have done.

"May I tell you a story?"

For an answer, she blew her nose loudly.

"It was in 1967," I began, realizing that the Christmas of 1967 was as remote to her as the first Christmas. "In early November we had word through the Red Cross that my brother Wesley was dead. His plane had crashed over North Vietnam two years before. He— he died in prison." For a minute the cold pain of Wesley's death returned. I had adored him.

"So?" she prompted, impatient to be done.

"It wasn't only that he was dead, but the way he died that hurt my father so. I think if he had been killed in the crash, my father would have been able to bear it. But it was the waste, the agony of his dying bit by bit in prison—"

"You do a lot of talk about dying," she said.

"Sorry. I'm trying to figure out why my father was so terribly bitter. He had always been a very religious man. He even named his sons after church heroes, but once he heard the news about Wesley, he stopped going to church, stopped saying grace at meals. He even tried to keep my mother from taking me and my sister to Sunday school. I was only nine. I couldn't understand."

"Easy," she said. "Sometimes you gotta pay God back."

"Well, Christmas came, and I was supposed to sing a solo in the Sunday school program. I was all excited about it, and so was my mother. I could tell that even my sister, who usually ignored me, was proud that I had been chosen. The night of the program my mother tried to persuade my father to go. I was a bit afraid of my father. I was worried that if he went he might be disappointed in me, so I wasn't sure I wanted him to go, but I wanted my mother to be happy. That was the real reason I wanted him to go."

"You should've left him alone."

"Yes, we should have, I guess. Anyhow, at suppertime my mother said that he owed it to me to go, that it was a big night in my life, and he would be proud to hear how well I sang. 'He can sing it right here in the kitchen for me,' my father said."

"You should've done it."

"I did. I stood there in the kitchen after supper

while he drank his coffee, and I sang for him. Do you know 'There's a Song in the Air'?"

"I don't know classical. I don't like it either."

"Don't worry. I won't sing it for you," I said. "But I sang it for him, and the more I sang, the more frightened I became. I could tell he was about to burst with rage. Even before I finished, he slammed his fist on the table and sloshed coffee all over the cloth. 'Lies!' he yelled. 'It's all lies!' Then he jumped up and grabbed me by the shoulders. He was like a crazy man. 'Don't you know what the world is like, Judson? There's no pretty angels flapping their wings. There's no singing in the sky. There's hate and suffering and cruel, cruel death!' Then he shoved me aside and grabbed my mother. 'I don't see it, Agnes. How you can hang onto all this nonsense! The air's not full of music. It's full of bombs crashing and people screaming!'

"My mother's face tightened, and she said very quietly, 'The song is louder.'

"My father began to curse. I had never heard him speak a word to my mother in anger, and now, all because of me, because I wanted to sing in the stupid Sunday school program, he was cursing her. I ran out of the house. It was a cold night, but it was a long time before I slowed down enough to notice. I was never going back. He had always despised me, I told myself. It was only for Wesley's sake that he had put up with me. Now Wesley was gone, so I was going, too. Before I knew it, I was deep in the woods, almost at the foot of that mountain over there, just as lost as I could be, and it was bitter cold."

"I take it you didn't freeze to death," she said sarcastically.

"No. I kept on walking, but it was a perfectly black night with no moon. I couldn't even see a tree before I bumped into it. I was terrified—all that trackless night. I was sure I was going to die out there in the cold dark all alone."

"Yeah," she said without a trace of sarcasm.

"And then, suddenly, I saw a light way off in the distance. I began to stumble toward it. It was the most wonderful thing I'd ever seen in my life, that light. I still couldn't see where I was walking, but it didn't matter. I just kept my eyes on the light."

"And you run smack into an angel of God Almighty."

"No. It was my father. He had come out to look for me."

"So he falls down on his knees and begs you to forgive him and you live happy ever after."

"No. I just went home with him. It was too late by then for any of us to go to the program. So that was that. We never spoke about it again."

"You can let me out here," she said. I hadn't realized that we were already at the edge of town.

"I don't like to just drop you off this time of night."

"No problem."

"Look. We're almost at the nursing home. Why don't you wait? As soon as I've seen my father, I'll take you home."

She made a sound, meant to be a laugh. "Don't do me any favors, mister."

I pulled up in front of the home. When I'd parked, I put on my wedding ring, took the money out of my wallet, and laid it on the front seat.

"I don't want your watch," she said. "You can take it."

"Thanks," I said. "Why don't you wait? I won't be but a minute, and then—"

She jerked her head in a nod.

"YOU'RE TOO LATE," Fran said. "He's not responding to anyone now."

I went to the bedside and took my father's big

hand. It was thinner than I'd remembered. He looked peaceful.

"He recognized me this afternoon," Fran said. "He spoke to me."

"Did he?" I was remembering the light, how he had come for me that night through the darkness.

"It didn't make much sense," she continued. "His voice was stronger than it's been for years. He said— 'Tell your mother the song is louder.' "

"I'll be right back," I said, almost running out. The car was empty. As I opened the front door to be sure, the light revealed a twenty-dollar bill on the seat. She hadn't wanted to leave me penniless.

I never saw her again. I could not tell her my father's last words. Not that she would have understood. But then, in a way, he was wrong. Both he and my mother were wrong. The song is not louder. It is swallowed up quickly in the cry of anger or the clack of greed. No, the song is not louder, but it persists. It comes, as it had come to me beside my father's bed, a melody of the most stubborn sweetness, for which we are never prepared. And we turn away from it again and again and again.

"But oh, my child," I said to the empty night,

"even though the song is not louder, it is stronger. And someday it will find you—out there alone in the darkness."

Then I turned and went back in to say good-bye to my father.

No Room
in the Inn

IN THE WINTER, our house looks like a Christmas card. It's an old Vermont farmhouse nestled into the woods, with a view of the snow-covered Green Mountains. The attached barn is now a garage, and my parents run a bed-and-breakfast in the house. My dad works full-time at a computer outfit, so, being both the only man and the only kid at home, I spend a lot of time splitting wood, making fires in the huge kitchen woodstove, cleaning rooms, changing sheets, washing dishes—you name it.

When I saw my parents off at Burlington Airport last week, I tried to look a little sad—as a Christmas present to my mother, who was feeling terrible about leaving me alone for the holidays. Can you imagine? An eighteen-year-old boy alone in a country inn with no guests to cater to, no wood to split, no beds to make—nothing to do for ten glorious days but eat, sleep, and ski. And a new Pontiac Grand Prix sitting in the other half of the garage whispering, "Use me! Use me! Use me!"

I had taken my folks to the airport in the 4 x 4. A good thing, too, because by the time I headed home, the snow was coming down hard. Great for the slopes, I thought, and switched on the radio, which was playing a sappy old-time number, "Let it Snow, Let it Snow, Let it Snow." I was feeling so good I listened to "White Christmas" and a jazzed-up version of "Away in a Manger" before I reached over to switch to my usual station. Ha! Ten days with no one complaining because I had switched the dial on the car radio.

I tried to figure out why I was feeling so great. Sure, I'd miss not having Christmas with the family. My sister's kids are terrific and they think their uncle Ben is God's gift to the world. But you have to understand. I never get time to myself these days. If I'm not working at school, I'm slaving away at the inn. It's really only a bed-and-breakfast, but my mother likes to call it The Inn. I'd have it all to myself, including the 4 x 4, which I have to share with my dad, and ta-da my mother's Pontiac, which for ten days was mine, all mine.

The euphoria had left me by the time I'd spent an hour and forty-five minutes driving what should have taken just over an hour. I was tired and hungry and feeling—could you believe it?—just a little bit sorry for myself in the blackness of a late winter afternoon when I turned off the interstate and headed for the village. I decided to stop at Gracie's, the only restaurant around for meat loaf and cheer. Gracie is famous for both.

The woodstove was crackling warm, and the smell of meat loaf and homemade bread filled the place. There were a couple of farmers, Ewell Biggs and Ames Whitehead, sitting at the counter drinking coffee when I got there. They nodded at me as I sat down. I nodded back, waiting for Gracie's usual "Hello, stranger!" But Gracie just stared at me sadly. "It's meat loaf tonight," she said, as though that would be the last thing anyone would want.

"That's fine," I said, and then, "is something the matter, Gracie?"

"Gracie's all worried about them Russians," Ewell explained to me between slurps of coffee.

"They're Armenians," Gracie said to him, and then to me, "I was just watching the news. Five hundred thousand with no place to sleep, and it's cold."

"It ain't like Vermont winter," Ames said. "Lord, it was seventeen below at my barn this morning."

"It's cold enough," Gracie insisted. "I saw this old woman on TV last night. They showed her hands. She was kinda holding them tight like this"—Gracie clutched her hands together in front of her ample bosom—"and she didn't have any gloves. She was just holding onto herself and shivering. It killed me. I couldn't sleep last night thinking about that poor old woman."

I thought Gracie was going to burst into tears, but she pulled herself together enough to get me a huge steaming plate of meat loaf, mashed potatoes, and beans, with three hot rolls on the side. She knows how I love her rolls.

Just then I felt a blast of air on my back. We all turned to look at the door. A man was standing there —a stranger. There was several days' growth of stubble on his face. He had on worn jeans and a flimsy baseball jacket and no hat or gloves. He was not anyone from around here.

"Take a seat," Gracie said. "Be right with you." Before I could ask for the ketchup, she was back to the Armenians. "And those children. Did you see those poor kids in the hospital with their legs all crushed? One little boy couldn't even remember who he was. The doctor didn't know if his parents were dead or alive."

I opened my mouth during the pause to ask for the ketchup, but by then she had turned to the stranger. "Now, what can I do for you?" she asked.

He was still standing in front of the door as though he couldn't remember what he'd come in for. "Coffee," he muttered at last. "To go."

"People who got through the earthquake are just freezing to death from the cold," Gracie went on as she filled a large Styrofoam cup from the coffee urn.

The man looked puzzled. "Armenians," I said. "She's all upset about the Armenians."

It was obvious he didn't know what we were talking about. "There was a big earthquake over there. They think about fifty to sixty thousand people died."

"And the rest are likely to." Gracie gave a huge

sigh. "Right at Christmas. I can't get over those poor children. Cream and sugar?"

"Yeah," the man said. "Both. Double."

Gracie put two teaspoons of sugar and a huge dollop of cream into the cup and pushed on a lid. "That'll be sixty-three cents," she said as the man handed her a dollar bill. "This mason jar here is for the Armenians," she said, pointing to it. "I'm taking donations—if you'd like to put in your change . . ."

The man took the change she held out and stuffed it into the pocket of his jeans. "How far to Burlington from here?" he asked.

"Well," said Gracie—you could tell she was a little bit annoyed that the man didn't care anything about her Armenians—"you get back on the interstate, it's about forty miles."

"I just came from there," I said, sticking my two cents in like a fool. "Road's terrible."

"Ah, they'll plow soon," said Ewell.

"I need gas," the man said.

"Well, that might be more of a problem. Nothing open this time of night," Ames said.

The man shrugged. He looked at Gracie, but she ignored him, carefully refilling my water glass. "Ben," she said. "You feeling lonely in that big place, come have Christmas dinner here with me."

"Thanks, Gracie," I said, keeping my back to the stranger. "I just might."

I felt the cold air as he opened the door to go. He muttered something as he went out. It sounded like "Damned Armenians," but maybe I just imagined that.

"Friendly soul," Ewell remarked.

"Not too worried about your Russians, either," Ames teased.

"Armenians," Gracie said looking sadder than ever, so when I was ready to go I stuffed all my change into the jar, even though I'd given her a twenty.

The first thing I did when I got back home was to hang out the NO VACANCY sign. I wasn't likely to get any visitors on a night like this, but I wasn't taking any chances. I had the evening all planned: first a roaring fire in the woodstove, then a large bottle of Coke and a two-pound bag of potato chips, then three rented videos in a row, none of which I would have been able to watch had there been anyone else in the house.

I had no sooner popped the first tape into the machine and settled back to watch when the doorbell rang . . . and rang . . . and rang. There was nothing to do but go answer. I put on the chain and opened the door a crack. "Sorry, no vacancy," I said, and then I saw it was the stranger from Gracie's.

"How about if I just stay in the garage?" he asked. "Like you said, the interstate is terrible, and it's freezing out here in the car."

It wasn't my problem. "Sorry," I said. "No vacancies. There's Woodley's just off the interstate."

"I already tried there," he said. "I ain't got sixty-five dollars."

"Well, if I could let you stay, which I can't, it's sixty-five here, too."

"Look, I'm just asking to stay in your garage, so I won't freeze to death. You'd let a stray dog into the garage, wouldn't you, night like this?"

I hesitated. I didn't really like his looks. Besides, the Pontiac was in there. If anything happened to that car, my mother would kill me.

He smiled then—the kind of shifty-eyed smile that immediately makes you distrust someone. "Just think of me as one of them Armenians," he said.

He was right. Fake smile or not, he *would* freeze to death in his car on a night like this. "Okay," I said. "Wait. I'll have to get my car out to make room for yours." I closed the front door and carefully locked it before going out through the kitchen to the attached garage. I got in the 4 x 4, pushed the button for the electric door, and slowly backed out. A ten-year-old Chevrolet with rusted sides drove into the slot beside the Pontiac. I got the old blankets out of the cargo area, then locked the 4 x 4 and hurried into the garage.

I put the blankets on the back of the Chevy. "Here's some blankets in case," I yelled as I pushed the button to close the door. I couldn't look at his old car. I couldn't think of the man out here when I had a roaring fire going in the kitchen. But I sure wasn't going to let him inside. People get robbed and beaten up for that kind of stupidity—murdered, even.

He didn't say anything, not even thanks. But it didn't matter. I gave him what he asked for—more than he asked for.

I went in and turned up the VCR very loud. . . . I don't know how long the knocking had been going on before I finally heard it. "Yeah?" I yelled through the closed kitchen door.

"Daddy said, could I use the bathroom?"

I was so startled to hear a kid's voice, I opened the door. Sure enough, there stood a dirty, skinny, red-faced kid. "Daddy said you'd let me use the bathroom."

I just opened the door wider and let him in. What

was I supposed to do? Tell the kid to go out in the snow? Sheesh. I shut the door behind him and led him to the downstairs powder room. "Don't use the towels," I warned.

I waited outside the bathroom for what seemed like ten minutes. What in the world was the kid up to? Finally, he came out, walking tall and straight backed like some little prince. He didn't say a word, not even thank you.

"You're welcome," I said loudly as I let him out the door, but he didn't look my way.

I just sat down. The guy hadn't said anything about any kid. I was sure he hadn't. I probably should call the welfare people or the police or somebody. I hadn't figured out what to do when there was another, softer knock on the kitchen door.

This time I just opened it. "You've been to the bathroom already," I started to say when I saw it was a different kid—a stringy-haired little girl with a runny nose rubbed raw. "Where did you come from?" I asked.

She whispered something.

"What?"

Again, I caught the word *bathroom*, so I shut the door and pointed her to the powder room. I didn't even bother to warn her about my mother's fancy guest towels. Somehow, I knew this was going to be a long night.

Before the kid had left the bathroom, there was another knock. I snatched open the door, all ready to give the guy a piece of my mind. But this time a woman stood there, holding a baby in a filthy rag of a blanket.

I couldn't believe it. This was like one of those circus acts where people just keep coming out of a car. "Would you warm it?" she asked. I looked down. She was handing me a baby bottle. It was about half full of frozen milk.

"You better do it," I said. I got her a saucepan, filled it with water, and turned on the burner. "The kid—the little girl's in the bathroom," I said, nodding in that direction. I waited, as patiently as I could, for the woman to test the milk on her wrist and shove the bottle into the baby's mouth, and for the little girl to finish wiping her grubby little hands on all four of Mom's embroidered Irish linen guest towels.

"Now," I said. "I'm very sorry, but you're going to have to go."

"It's cold out there," the little girl whined as I tried to gently urge her out the door.

"I know," I said grimly, going out with her around the Pontiac toward the Chevy. The man was sitting there behind the wheel, with all the windows rolled up. I went to the driver's side and tapped, but he didn't roll the window down. He looked straight ahead. I banged louder. "You're going to have to go," I said. "This isn't going to work. You didn't tell me you had kids with you."

The man turned slowly and opened the window a crack. He gave me a look—it was the most sarcastic expression I've ever seen on a man's face. "Just pretend we're some of them Armenians," he said and rolled the window up again.

I stood there for a minute, trying to figure out what to do next. It was so quiet I could hear the soft sounds of the baby drinking its milk. The little girl was watching me from the other side of the Chevy with big scared eyes. The woman hadn't moved. She was still standing in the doorway, the baby cradled in her arms, a dark silhouette against the light streaming from the bright kitchen. ". . . 'Round yon Virgin Mother and Child . . ." A shiver went through me.

"I'm sorry," I said to her, and I really was. It wasn't her fault. "I'm sorry, but you're going to have to find someplace else. I don't own this place. I'm just taking care of it, and the owners wouldn't approve of me letting people stay in the garage."

No one moved, but the little girl began to whimper again.

"I think there's a shelter or something in Barre. I could call on the phone . . ." Still no one moved.

I went back to the kitchen door and pressed the opener button on the wall.. The garage light flashed on and the door rattled up. The woman jumped, and the little girl started crying in earnest. "I'm sorry," I said again, although I was beginning to feel more angry than sorry. That jerk had really taken advantage.

Just pretend we're some of them Armenians. The nerve. I watched the woman help the crying child into the backseat of the car and climb in after her. The baby's blanket caught on something and she jerked it free. I could hear a tearing sound. At the front window the boy sat, his nose flattened against the pane.

I waited but nothing happened. The man was just going to sit there. Anger washed away what guilt I might have felt. I went around to the man's window again. "If you don't move out of here," I said, "I'm calling the police."

The man acted as if he hadn't heard. Suppose he just stayed there and they all froze to death right in our garage? Imagine the headlines—NO ROOM IN THE INN: HOMELESS FAMILY FREEZES AT LOCAL B & B. "I'm not kidding," I shouted. "I'm calling the cops!"

Through the closed windows of the Chevy, I could hear the little girl crying. "Come on!" I yelled to block out the sound. "Get outta here!"

Finally, he started the motor and began to back out slowly. I ran to the 4 x 4. As soon as the Chevy was out of the way, I was going to drive it in and close the door. The snow had stopped. The plows would be out soon. They'd be okay. An unheated barn was no place for a baby.

And then I heard myself. "Away in a manger, no crib for his bed." No room in the inn, not for two thousand lousy years. Never.

The Chevy had stalled in the driveway. I jumped out and ran to the driver's window and pounded on it again. He stopped grinding the starter and turned to give me his sarcastic look. "We're going," he said.

"I changed my mind."

Now he opened the window. "What you say?"

"Put your car back in and come on in the house. It's freezing out here."

He smiled grimly. "Thinking about them Armenians, huh?"

"No," I said. "Actually, I was thinking about something else."

I led the way into the kitchen and found them chairs so they could sit around the stove and get warm. Then I went to the phone to call Gracie. I knew I needed help, and she was sure to come. I'd just tell her I had a houseful of Armenians.

Poor Little Innocent Lamb

ISAIAH HAD PITIED the child before he ever lay eyes on her. Anyone who had to come live with Old Lettie was to be pitied, but when he saw her climbing down off the Greyhound, the last step almost too much for her skinny little white legs, his heart went out to her as it did to one of his hurt and helpless creatures. They weren't his creatures, of course. It wasn't his farm. It was Old Lettie's farm, but she never went out the door of the farmhouse to tend to it. She just nursed the account books, as though numbers on paper were a farm. So although he was only the hired man, it was, in actual fact, his farm, and all the creatures were his to care for.

Except this one getting off the bus—this poor little girl, dark, stringy hair past her narrow shoulders, and deep, sad eyes. Her face was streaked with dirt—tears, he thought at the time, though later he wondered. The child never cried.

"So," he said, when he had settled her and her tiny vinyl suitcase into the cab of the pickup. "So—you Miss Lettie's grandniece, eh? I got a passel of grand-nieces and -nephews myself."

There was no answer. Maybe she wasn't at ease with black folks. He tried again. "I told you already my name's Isaiah, but you ain't told me your name."

She was kicking the seat rhythmically with the back of her legs, staring straight ahead.

"Look," he said, starting the motor and watching the rearview mirror as he backed carefully out of the Greyhound parking lot. "I'll tell you right off, it might be kinda lonely for you out on the farm. Miss Lettie don't go out, and the animals aren't big talkers. Now, I live over the garage and you may figure I'm just the hired help, but I expect I'll be the best company around. If you don't make friends with me, it's likely to be mighty lonesome for you."

She looked at him sideways, and, for a moment, stopped her kicking. "Travis," she said.

"Huh?"

"It's my name. Travis."

He didn't tell her he'd never heard of such a fool name for a little girl. But then, any mother fool enough to ship a baby like this off to live with the very aunt she'd run off from when she was a girl was likely to saddle her poor child with some crazy name. Isaiah thought of his own loving mother, who had given each of her eight children a name from the Bible so that they could grow up straight and proud. She still fussed over him as she had when he was tiny—and he sixty years old come February.

He thought of his sisters and brothers and nieces and nephews and all their children, tumbling in and out of one another's lives in noisy, happy confusion. He turned and smiled at this little deserted thing beside him to show that he didn't hold her name against her, but she kept staring straight ahead, even though she couldn't see over the dashboard, and never looked his way.

"Well," he said at last. "Here we are." He got out and opened the gate, drove through, and got out again to close it. They rattled up the graveled drive to the old farmhouse. It was a huge, white frame, which had been added to and taken away from for a hundred years or more until Old Lettie's father finally wrapped it around with porches and gingerbread trim, putting an end to all his ancestors' tinkering. Isaiah drove the pickup around to the back as usual. "You'd best go in at the front," he told the child as he leaned across her to open the door. "I'll bring your bag."

She climbed down and followed the direction of his head around the west porch and the pyracantha bushes to the front door. He got her bag. It was too light to hold anything worth having. Lucille should have sent some warm clothes with the child. Lord have mercy. He shook his head. Poor little innocent lamb.

She was waiting at the front door. "It's locked," she said.

"Nah, ain't locked. Just got to yank hard," he said, pulling the heavy door open for her. "I expect Miss Lettie's upstairs. Little sitting room at the top of the staircase . . ." That mean old thing. She could at least come down to welcome the poor little scared creature. She could've gone to the bus station if she'd had half an ounce of kindness about her.

All she did when she got the news was rant about how no 'count Lucille was and how no 'count Lucille's mother Mildred had been, and how her whole life was plagued with nothing but no 'count bums, including him, Isaiah Washington. He'd nearly taken off on the spot. The only thing that kept him around enduring her insults year after year was the animals. If he left, what would become of the poor creatures?

He followed the child, her sneakered feet dragging as she went down the long dark hall, past the huge mirrored coat-and-umbrella stand on the left, the mahogany table with the plastic flower arrangement on the right. She paused a second, just to touch the flowers, and then, clinging to the right side of the hallway, she made her way to the foot of the long staircase. She took a deep breath and started up, holding onto the banister as if to pull herself along. He stood below, waiting to hear what the old woman would say. At last the child crossed the threshold into the room.

"So you're Travis." The shrill angry voice traveled down the stairs. "What kind of a name is that supposed to be?" As though the child were to blame. As though the child, long before she was born, had made first her grandmother and then her mother run away from this house. As though the child had chosen to come here to torment the bitter old woman.

"You look like your mother. Same wild-looking eyes . . . Well, don't just stand there staring. Can't you see I'm busy? Some of us do our duty . . ."

He wanted to run and pick up that suitcase and whack that mean old face. Instead, he called to the child and took her downstairs to the tiny bedroom off the kitchen and put her little suitcase on the bed. There were bigger, grander rooms in the old house, but none that would be as warm. And he had known even before he saw her that she would need to have a warm little nest in this cold house. All winter he kept a fire going in the big iron stove. He would take care of her. Of all the creatures God had given him to tend, he pitied her the most.

IT WAS HE who took the child to town and bought her warm pants to cover her thin legs. It was he who enrolled her in the county school. If it rained, he always managed to be at the stop in the pickup when the bus door opened.

The child never thanked him. Not because she was rude, but because since that first day she hardly spoke at all. The house was as quiet with the child living in it as it had been with only the old woman. Isaiah did the cooking, as he had for years now, and sometimes Old Lettie would leave her account books and deign to come to the kitchen table. Most often she demanded that he bring the meal up to her. Her life had not been changed by the presence of the child.

The child seemed to sense that she was not to bother her grandaunt. She almost tiptoed about the house, and when they were at the table together, she was as silent as a doll baby, hardly eating for fear it might disturb. Sometimes, when she thought her aunt wasn't looking, she would stare at the old woman with her big, sorrowful eyes. It nearly broke Isaiah's heart to see.

He had never had any children of his own, but he was awash in grandnieces and -nephews. He spent his Sundays being crawled over by children. They were noisy, happy, naughty children, frisky as young lambs. It wasn't right, he knew, for a child of eight to be so quiet.

ONE DAY WHEN she was at school, he determined to speak to Old Lettie about it. She was the child's grandaunt, after all, whether she had chosen to be or not. He found her hunched over the account books in her little sitting room. The door was open, but he knocked anyway.

"What's the matter?" she snapped. "Haven't you got work to do?"

"Miss Lettie, I got to talk to you."

"Well, make it quick."

"That child's about to starve."

"Don't be ridiculous."

"She's starving for notice. If you'd just talk to her. Pay her a little mind."

"You pay a mind to your affairs, Isaiah, and leave me to pay a mind to mine. By the way, I hope you're remembering that the price you got for lamb last spring was twenty-five cents *less* than you got the year before. You'll have to do better than that."

"Yes ma'am," he said, determining that Travis would be his to pay mind to from then on. But he couldn't do it alone. "Lord," he prayed, "you got to help me save this baby girl."

He began to talk to her all the time she was about. It didn't matter that she didn't answer or didn't even seem to listen half the time. He was determined to talk her ear off. He hadn't realized how hard talking was. He often ran out of things to say and had to repeat himself. He told her Bible stories and stories about when he was a little boy. He even took to buying a newspaper when he went to town so he could talk to her about the news.

"And this man sold his business and they gave him a check for fifty-six thousand dollars to pay for it, and his dog *ate the check!*" The two of them were peeling potatoes. Travis didn't look up from her spud. He nudged her. "His dog ate the check right down. Now that check was for thousands. That's his whole life's work right down the gullet of his poodle. Now what was he gonna do? He calls up the bank and says: 'My dog done ate up my check. Would you kindly write me another one?' 'Course they think the fellow is crazy in the head or trying to cheat 'em, one or the other. So they say he got to bring proof. Well, ain't but one way to bring proof . . ."

Suddenly he realized that he'd gotten himself further into the story than he'd meant to. After all, she was just a little girl. He cleared his throat. "Well, I guess you wouldn't want to know about that . . ."

"I swallowed a nickel once." Her solemn voice was hardly louder than a whisper.

"Sure enough?"

"Yeah," she said. "The doctor at the clinic said you just have to wait."

"That's right. That's just what the man had to do."

Had he imagined it, or had she actually smiled at her potato?

IT WAS LATE November when he realized that the Lord was answering his prayer. One of his old ewes was going to give birth out of season, and from the size of her he guessed it might be twins. He brought her into the garage so he would be close by if she needed him. The twins were born one cold night. The first struggled quickly to its wobbly legs and began to nurse as soon as the ewe would let him. But when the second one, the runty one, tried to join her brother, he butted her away. The old ewe walked to the far side of the garage with her firstborn close behind. The little one just stood there bleating, too weak to follow.

Isaiah wrapped her in an old car robe and carried her to the warm kitchen. He always kept a baby bottle handy and he fetched it from the shelf. He had his head in the refrigerator getting out the milk when he heard Travis's bare feet pattering on the linoleum.

"What's the matter?" she asked sleepily.

He took out the milk and poured some into a saucepan, nodding as he did so at the blanket-wrapped lamb in the rocking chair. "It was twins, and the old ewe can't take care of both. So she sent this one over to you."

"To me?" Her eyes went wide.

"Yep. I'm fixing a bottle right now. Then you got to do it from now on. I'll feed her while you're at school, but I'm too busy to bother otherwise. You got to take care of her for me."

Travis walked over to the chair, from which came such piteous little bleats that Isaiah himself could hardly bear to listen. "Hush," she whispered. "Don't cry. Travis is going to take care of you."

Travis kept the lamb in a box in her room. They didn't tell Old Lettie it was in the house. It was their secret. At last they had something real to talk about, and Travis began to talk. She named the lamb Orphan Annie and fussed over it like a little old mother. To Isaiah's delight and relief, the lamb responded, growing strong and mischievous, like a young creature should. The man and the child never minded cleaning up after it. They scolded, of course, but instantly forgave. And Travis would immediately undo the effects of any scolding by petting and hugging and reassuring the lamb that they only spoke harshly because Old Lettie mustn't know, mustn't be upset.

The child was not only talking to him, she was smiling. Isaiah thanked the Lord every day for that mean old ewe and her troublesome lamb.

For Christmas he helped Travis buy a collar for the lamb. He also bought a little net stocking filled with chocolate candy covered with gold paper and a huge candy cane. Old Lettie had never celebrated Christmas in the years he had worked for her, so he could not count on her even remembering the date, and he wanted Travis to have something from Santa Claus.

After the Christmas Eve service at his church, which was near Bethel on the other side of the county, Isaiah always went on to spend Christmas with his old mother, so he took special pains to fix a nice dinner for the child on Christmas Eve. She helped him in every way she could, even getting the plastic flowers from the hall table to make a special centerpiece. He found some candles and lit them. Travis ran to switch off the ceiling light.

"My, that's pretty, ain't it?" he said.

In the candlelight her face seemed to glow. "You think Miss Lettie will like it?" she asked shyly.

"Sure to," he said, though he'd never known the old woman to like anything but a large profit. "Tell you what," he said. "I'll go up and make sure she comes down for supper tonight. You get Annie to the garage."

He found Old Lettie in her usual chair, not, for once, studying her books—just sitting there in the dark.

"Supper's ready, Miss Lettie," he said.

"I don't feel up to coming down."

"Just this once. It's Christmas and the child's got everything fixed up nice for you."

She had opened her mouth, probably to refuse, when it happened. There was a clatter and cry and crash after crash. Isaiah took the stairs five at a time, but it was too late. Their beautiful dinner was a jumble of broken china and glass all over the kitchen floor. Annie was standing there, the end of the tablecloth still in her tiny black mouth. Travis was holding the candles. "Nothing's on fire," she said and burst into tears.

"Now, now," he said. "It can't be all that bad." But when he pulled the light cord, it was hard to see how it might be worse.

He soon saw how. If the invitation had not brought Old Lettie down to join them, the sounds of disaster had.

"What's going on?" she cried. "What is that animal doing in my house? Wrecking everything I own?"

"Just go on back upstairs, Miss Lettie," Isaiah said.

"I'll get this cleaned up in no time. Travis, you best get the lamb outside."

"I don't know where that animal came from, but I know where it's going tomorrow!" the old woman shouted. "It's going to the slaughterhouse if I have to carry it there myself. What's going on in that head of yours, Isaiah? Letting that animal into my house. Hasn't my life been upset enough?"

Travis, her face white as the tablecloth, picked up the lamb. She staggered, adjusting to its weight. It was almost too heavy for her now. "Best take her to the barn," he said quietly under the old woman's raving.

"She can't kill Annie," the child whispered.

"Of course I can kill it. What do you think we raise sheep for around here, you foolish child? For slaughter—for market—so we can live."

Travis turned and stumbled out the back door with Annie in her arms. Isaiah let Lettie carry on while he cleaned the floor on his hands and knees. She would run down eventually. When she did, she fell exhausted into the rocking chair.

The kitchen was in order, but Travis had not come back in. The old woman was rocking agitatedly.

"I best go out and find the child." He was almost too angry with her to speak, and it was a struggle to keep his voice even. "If you get hungry, there's some cold cuts in the refrigerator."

He grabbed his jacket and flashlight and slammed out the back door. When there was no sign of Travis in the barn or shed, he went to the garage. He shone his flashlight on the old blanket in the back of the pickup. It had two humps under it, and one of them was wriggling, nervous as a snake. Isaiah hopped into the cab and started down the highway. After several miles, he heard a little tapping at the rear window of the cab. He looked into the mirror to see two noses pressed against the glass. He hoped he looked very surprised. At any rate, he stopped and ran around to the back to help his stowaways down. "Best come up front where it's warm," he said.

Travis, shivering like a newborn calf, didn't argue. She just climbed up on the seat, hugging Annie close.

He carefully shifted gears and pulled out into the road. "Where you two fixing to go?"

"Away."

"I see. Any particular place in mind?"

"California."

"Where your momma is?"

"I was only here temporary, you know. Just till she got settled."

"Sure."

"But I can't wait no more."

"Not like that man and his old poodle, huh?"

She didn't smile at his joke. "Lettie's too mean. How come my momma sent me to stay with somebody so mean and hateful?"

"I don't know," he said. He couldn't understand it himself. Couldn't Lucille remember why she ran away? "I guess she was kind of desperate. She figured Old Lettie for all her meanness would try to do her duty by you."

"I don't want to be her duty. It's miserable to be her duty."

He sighed. "Yeah, but you got to figure she's pretty miserable, too."

"Well, she can just be miserable all by herself. I'm not going to help her anymore."

He drove on for a while in silence, the headlights blinking up and down the bumpy road.

"Where you going?" she asked finally.

"Well, I'm due over to my church. All my relatives there give this big Christmas play and they're expecting me to join them. After that I'll go on into Bethel and say good-bye to my poor old momma. Then I'm fixing to run away, too."

"You can't do that!"

"Who says I can't?"

"Grown-ups don't run away. They go to California to find themselves."

"Well, I didn't know I was lost, but, whatever . . . Anyhow, since none of us is planning to go back there, why don't you come along with me—just for this evening?"

"They won't allow Annie in church."

"What d'you mean? That dumb sheep'll steal the show."

AND OF COURSE she did. Bethel Church had never had a live lamb abiding in the fields before. After the songs of men and angels and women and little children, the Angel Gabriel himself (who looked a lot like Isaiah Washington) told the shepherds (one of whom was female and dressed in a man's lumber jacket instead of a bathrobe) to get themselves over to Bethlehem and find that little baby boy lying in a manger and "take that no 'count little lamb along. If ever there was a sinful creature in need of God's salvation, she's the one."

The happy shepherds giggled, but they obeyed and took Annie all the way to Bethlehem to the feed box, in which lay Isaiah's grandnephew, Elroy, aged seven months. Annie went right over and began to nibble the straw, accidentally nuzzling the baby, who laughed out loud, which made everyone laugh and clap and burst joyfully into the final carol. Afterward they crowded around Travis and Isaiah and Annie to thank them for helping Bethel Church to have such a fine Christmas play.

Suddenly Travis had an idea. They would take the entire cast over to sing for Old Lettie. They would bring Bethlehem to her whether she wanted it or not. Isaiah wasn't sure it was such a good notion, and his relatives were even less sure, but Travis begged, and Annie let out the most pitiful bleat they ever heard in their lives. So they piled into cars and trucks and drove back across the county to the dark old house on the hill. They began singing along the road, and they were still singing when they got out at the house. They stood and sang on the sagging porch under the gingerbread trim, but there was no sign from the house that anyone was listening.

Travis ran to the door and *blam*med the heavy knocker with all her might.

"No, no," Old Lettie called out from just inside. "Don't come in. I don't want you to come in. Haven't

I been upset enough?" But Travis would not be stopped. She pulled the heavy door wide and ordered Isaiah and all the relatives and friends to follow her to the kitchen. Old Lettie trailed after them, sputtering like a faulty faucet.

Travis pushed her old aunt gently into the rocking chair beside the stove.

"Seems like we're going to do a little play for you, Miss Lettie," said Isaiah as he leaned down and put his laughing baby nephew into the old woman's lap.

She gave a little shriek. "Don't!"

"Careful!" Travis cried. "You'll drop the Baby Jesus!"

" 'There's a star in the east on Christmas morn!' " Isaiah's powerful baritone boomed out, and all the cast replied: " 'Rise up, shepherd, and follow!' "

" 'It will lead to the place where Christ was born,' " he sang. " 'Rise up, shepherd, and follow!' " they echoed.

Travis smiled and hugged her lamb, while tears poured down Old Lettie's face onto the child on her lap. And whether they were tears of anger or tears of joy didn't matter to Isaiah just then. It was Christmas. At least for this little while, heaven and nature were singing and all the lost lambs of the world had been found.

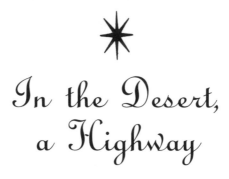

In the Desert, a Highway

KO-KO-KO. A pause, then—*ko-ko-ko.* The knock was no louder than a whisper. Comrade Wong looked at her watch and sighed. Every night at fifteen minutes past twelve, Old Lee tapped his special knock on her dormitory door. And every night when she opened the door, there stood the college night watchman in his faded blue jacket and trousers with a ragged book under his arm, asking her to read to him.

It was dangerous reading the Christian book aloud in the middle of the night. But once last winter a wind had blown out the flame in her kerosene heater. Old Lee on his nightly rounds had smelled the fumes and carried her unconscious body to safety. She had been grateful. She owed him her life, so she had said rashly, "If there is anything I can do for you, comrade . . ."

The next night he had appeared at her door with the book under his arm. "I am a Christian," he had said in his hoarse voice, "but I am an ignorant man and I cannot read the Book."

"Why don't I teach you?" The old man's eyesight was poor and his brain stiff. He could remember a few words, but Chinese characters are intricately made and easily forgotten, even by an agile mind. By summer she gave up all pretense of teaching and simply read to him.

He wanted to begin at the beginning. He marveled over the tales of Genesis. The laws of Exodus and Leviticus had been something of a trial to them both. The rituals of the Hebrews seemed barbaric to Comrade Wong. Once in a while she tried to point out how primitive all these rules were, but Lee simply shook his old head, the gray bristly hair sticking up like dry grass.

"Just read," he said. "Please, sister, just read what it says."

So she'd read on through Numbers and Deuteronomy until she finally got the foolish Israelites out of the wilderness, only in Judges to have them sink into degradation worse than the times before the flood.

"Look at your heroes! They are full of pride and lust and greed," she protested.

He listened gravely as she read of the evil doings of Gideon and Samson and the sons of Samuel, and the mad ravings of Saul the King. When the Book told of David's adultery and murderous act, she thought she saw tears on the old man's face, but he urged her to keep reading.

The best parts were the Psalms. As a teacher of literature, she liked the poetry, and the old man drank in the words of comfort. They both pretended to ignore the demands of the poets that God slaughter their enemies. It was hard to know exactly who one's enemies were these days. There was great unrest in the city. The two of them did not mention it, but deep inside herself, Comrade Wong was afraid.

By the time the young hoodlums who called themselves Red Guards invaded the campus, Comrade Wong and Old Lee had gotten to Ecclesiastes: "Vanity, vanity, all is vanity . . ." How could all of her ideals be vanity? She had tried with her whole heart to support the revolution. She lived very simply, owning nothing aside from her worn blue garments and a few books, all of which had been approved for their revolutionary thought. She had never married, choosing instead to give her life to teaching the young—to making China a strong and respected nation in the world.

Now these mobs were invading the college grounds, breaking windows, setting fire to library books, until finally some of the students and professors fought back, drove the invaders out, and padlocked the gate against them.

Ko-ko-ko. Silence. *Ko-ko-ko.* Not tonight. Tonight she must decide how to hide her books so they would not be destroyed. She went to the door and cracked it. He stood there but without his book. "I won't keep you long, sister," he said. "But it is getting cold, and I noticed the soles of your shoes are very thin."

"I don't have coupons to buy new shoes," she said. "Times are very hard. We must all bear these minor discomforts for the sake of the revolution."

He nodded. "I made some padded linings for you. If you'll let me borrow your shoes, I'll fit the linings and return your shoes before morning."

"You mustn't bother yourself, comrade. There are others far worse off than I."

"But you have been so kind," he said. "I wanted to make you a small gift"—he gave his sweet, nearly toothless smile—"for Christmas."

She stiffened. The man would get her into trouble yet.

"Would you accept a New Year's gift?" He was like a child, trying so hard to please. How could she offend him?

She handed him her shoes. They were worn straight through as he had observed. "Thank you for your kindness, comrade . . ."

When she opened her door early the next morning, the shoes were there with their new cloth linings and a bright coat of polish. Fortunately they were old and stretched, or the thick new inner soles would have made them too small. They were snug, but the stone floor was no longer so cold beneath her feet.

She crept to the community washroom while it was still dark. She had arisen before dawn because she had to hide her books. When the mob came back, as they surely would, they would finish destroying the library and then ransack the teachers' rooms, destroying whatever threatened them. She had no antiques, no jewelry, not even any banned books. But she did have her literature books. These young zealots were putting out the word that all scholars and students were in fact enemies of the true revolution—that the only book that a true revolutionary needed was the book of Chairman

Mao's thoughts. Any other book would lead to false philosophies.

She ripped open her bed quilt and stuffed the small paperback volumes in the middle of the cotton padding. Quickly she sewed the quilt back up. Her fingers were shaking. Although her breath came out in white puffs in the cold room, she perspired as she worked. What about her larger books? Her dictionary? Her anthology of poetry? Feverishly she gathered them up. They were an awkward, heavy load, but she hurried to the night watchman's door. It was open.

"Sister," he said. "Good morning. Do your new linings fit?"

"They are a great help. Thank you," she said. "May I come in?"

He stepped aside. The room was so tiny that even his meager belongings made it look crowded. "I want to ask you a great favor," she said, looking about for a hiding place.

"Of course, sister." His grin showed his toothless gums.

"Could you—would you hide my books in here? No one would think to look for books in your room."

He grinned even wider than before. "You're right.

Everyone knows how ignorant I am." He took the books from her. "Hurry," he said. "The others will be up soon. I'll take care of these for you."

THE MOB RETURNED about noon. This time there were party officials in the lead and police all around. "We have heard that subversive materials have been harbored here," the local party chairman said.

Faculty and students were herded to the athletic field while the Red Guards went through all the buildings and dormitories. A bonfire was kindled in the midst of the soccer field. Antique furniture, scrolls, and books were brought out and thrown onto the flames. Those in whose rooms the objects were found were separated from the rest of the community. The chairman wrote their names in his notebook.

A great shouting arose. Two of the mob had gone into the night watchman's room, where he pretended to be sleeping. When they tried to drag him out, he clung to the quilts. They were suspicious, and sure enough, the old man was lying on a bed of subversive books. They lifted the books in the air, one by one, before they threw them into the fire.

"See the evil eggs the old one has been trying to hatch!" a young woman screamed.

"The rest of you we only warn," the chairman cried out. "This enemy of the people must be made an example of."

Comrade Wong watched in horror as they stripped off Old Lee's ragged jacket and began to beat him with a thin bamboo stick. She thought a scream would surely escape from her lips each time the stick whacked down on the old man's back. What should she do? Those were her books. He had hidden them for her. Surely he would tell them that.

The college president stepped out from the group and went over to the chairman. "There is some mistake," he said. "Comrade Lee does not know how to read."

A young guard slammed a dunce cap on President Shen's head. He commanded the president to march around the bonfire shouting, "I am a fool! I am a fool!" The mob jeered and screamed with laughter. At last the fire burned out. The teachers and students were dismissed.

The next day Comrade Wong learned that both the president and the night watchman had been taken away. Most of the students packed their bags and went home. "It is nearly the New Year's holiday," they said. The teachers left as well. Comrade Wong had no home to go to—no relatives who would take her in.

NIGHT AND DAY she listened for the Red Guards to return. She nursed her fear, because somehow she knew that if she let go of it, even a little, she would be overwhelmed by shame. It was she who had caused the night watchman to be beaten and the president disgraced—both of them to be arrested.

She was almost relieved when the mob came back again, for this time they found the books she had sewn into her quilt and took her away too. She was put in a cattle car with more than thirty other women. Some were prostitutes and thieves, some teachers like herself, others simple women who had no notion what their crime might be.

By the time the doors were flung open again and they were ordered to climb out, the women were filthy and weak to the point of illness. Even the pale winter sun blinded their eyes.

Before them stretched a treeless plain as far as they could see. They must have traveled hundreds of miles into the interior. They stumbled from the train to a line of wooden barracks in the middle of a field. There they were at last given water for washing themselves and ordered to come to the dining hall to eat.

"At dawn you will begin work," said a young man, who seemed to be the leader. "We are building a road where no road has ever been built before. To honor the revolution and our beloved chairman, we have the privilege of building a great new highway."

We are too weak to walk, Comrade Wong thought, how can we build a road? But she did as she was told and stumbled to the dining hall. The food was poor, a kind of gruel made of millet, but she ate it. She must regain her strength—if she did not struggle, she would die in this desolate place. She was dimly aware that the hall was crowded. They were not the first workers to be brought here.

She left the table when she finished her gruel, washed her bowl and chopsticks at the common sink, and followed the crowd of women through the darkness to the barracks. She fell asleep at once and dreamed she heard a knocking at the door—*ko-ko-ko* . . . *ko-ko-ko*. She sat bolt upright on the wooden cot and listened, but all she heard was the breathing of the women around her.

The next day, as she carried a basket of gravel from the pit to the roadway, she saw him. He was pulling a heavy roller used to smooth the road surface. His face was thinner than she remembered. The night watchman must be at least ten years older than she. Now he looked thirty years older. She went as close to him as she dared.

"I trust that Comrade Lee is in good health," she murmured.

He jerked his head up at her voice and grinned his sweet, toothless smile. "It warms this old heart to see my sister's face once more," he said.

She smiled and nodded her head in a bow. How like him to continue calling her sister—a prerevolutionary greeting. She was absurdly glad to see him. Later that same morning she came upon President Shen as well. He acknowledged her with a stiff nod.

SHE BEGAN LOOKING for them every day. Old Lee would smile across the dining hall at her or nod on the construction site. Despite the poor food and heavy work, she was not unhappy. At the reeducation meeting one night, she confessed to the other women in her little group that she had been a selfish intellectual who had not understood the contribution of the masses to the rebuilding of China. But here, working on the road, she felt she had become a true revolutionary, able at last to understand the teachings of Chairman Mao. She was very grateful.

The group leader was pleased. One day the project head called her to his office—a tiny shack almost filled with an oversized desk. "Comrade Wong," he said, "your confession serves as a fine example to the other women. You are to be congratulated."

"I only spoke what is true," she said. "I am happy to serve the revolution in this place."

She was asked to repeat her confession for several other reeducation groups. At first she was glad to do so, but the night she spoke to a men's group and saw Old Lee and President Shen sitting there, she was embarrassed. They were in this place because of her. Old Lee smiled when she came in, his face so thin that it was like the grin of a skull. The president nodded, but he did not smile.

Usually her confession tumbled out like a waterfall, but tonight she stumbled and had to repeat words. She was relieved when it was finally done and she was permitted to leave. She was afraid the project manager would scold her for her poor performance, but instead, as they walked back toward her barracks, he said, "In the group tonight there were two men from your former college, I believe."

"Yes, comrade."

"I hope they will learn from your example."

"They work hard," she said. "I see them on the road. They are good workers, comrade."

"Oh, yes," he said. "They work hard enough. But I see no signs of their renouncing their former counterrevolutionary activity." The leader was fishing for something. "You are aware, I'm sure, that the old one was arrested for hiding right-wing books, and that the younger one was arrested for seeking to defend the wrongdoer."

"I—I heard something of the sort."

"We want you to use your influence with them—persuade them to confess."

She was glad it was dark so that he could not see her face. "I don't see how I could be of any help, comrade."

"You are wrong. The old one obviously respects you. I saw his warm greeting. And it is well known that the younger one cares a great deal for the old one. We are going to give you separate housing, comrade," the leader continued. "Then your former colleagues can visit you. You can talk to them, show them the virtue of confessing their past errors and embracing with a full heart the teachings of our chairman.''

So Comrade Wong was given a little shack of her own and a new, bright red copy of the teachings of Chairman Mao. No longer did she have to carry baskets of gravel. She was a supervisor on the road. But not even she knew where the road was going. It began abruptly in the middle of nowhere, and they were building it inch by inch toward the setting sun.

Old Lee continued to pull a roller. It was work for an ox or a mule, but they had neither. The president was one of the men who raked the gravel in an even layer after it was dumped on the roadway by the women. Sometimes, if he finished raking before a new load arrived, he would run to where Old Lee was straining at the roller's ropes and help the old man pull. Perhaps, as supervisor, Comrade Wong should have reprimanded him for leaving his own post, but she did not.

One evening after supper the two of them appeared at her door. As always, Old Lee smiled broadly at the sight of her. The president's face was stern. It was he who spoke.

"The project leader said you wished to see us."

So, the time had come. She stepped aside to let them enter her room. There was only one chair. She motioned for the president to sit on it, but he nodded for Old Lee to take the chair and he himself sat down on the floor. Old Lee grinned, shook his head, and sat down on the floor as well. Comrade Wong perched on the edge of her cot and stared at the empty chair. She did not know how to begin.

"This brings back happy times," the old man said. "Miss Wong tried to teach me to read, you know."

"No," said the president. "I did not know." He looked a bit less stern.

Now he will tell, thought Comrade Wong, wondering who might be listening outside the door, but the old man said nothing more.

She stared at the beaten earth floor of her little shack. How could she persuade them to confess when it was her wrongdoing for which they had been brought to this place of exile?

At last the president said, "Comrade Wong, I think it is your duty to speak to us about reeducation. Comrade Lee and I are suspected of harboring right-wing religious beliefs."

She looked up in surprise.

"After he was taken to the police station and

stripped, they found pages of the Christian Bible sewn up in his padded jacket," he said. "Of course, he would never have been taken to the station if"—his voice dropped to a whisper—"if it were not for the books found in his room."

Her face was hot. "If you would only say in your reeducation group that your past thinking was mistaken and that you are eager to be reeducated . . ." She heard the pleading tone in her voice and felt shame.

"How can an old fool like me be reeducated, sister? I was never educated to begin with."

"Perhaps," said the president, "he could tell how he came to have right-wing books in his room."

"Yes," Comrade Wong said weakly, "he could do that."

"I can't confess to having right-wing books in my room. How can I know if a book is right wing, left wing, or tail wing? I can't read a character. You know that as well as anyone, sister."

"Comrade."

"Oh, yes. Comrade."

"You see, Comrade Wong. Your cause is hopeless. Tell the project leader you tried, but it is hopeless," said the president.

"But what about you, Comrade Shen? Surely you are not hopeless."

"I was detained and sent here for reeducation because I made an inflammatory public statement: 'Comrade Lee does not know how to read.' How can I repent for saying publicly what is absolutely true?"

"Perhaps there is something in your past life, unrelated to Comrade Lee . . ." She did not ask him if he had ever been a Christian. She did not ask them anything for fear they would think her an informer.

"Good night, comrade," the president was saying. "I am sorry we have been such trouble to you." She could tell by his eyes that he already considered her an informer.

"IT WILL TAKE TIME," she told the project leader. "The old one is a hard-headed peasant and the younger one feels a certain loyalty to him."

Comrade Wong suggested a human chain for passing baskets of gravel from the pit to the roadway, which made the procedure more efficient. She was declared "People's Hero" for the month of August. Otherwise, August was a terrible month. The heat burned the crops in the fields and there was no rain.

She saw Old Lee fall down. She was sure it was heatstroke and told President Shen and another worker to carry him to the barracks and take care of him. When he came back to work the next morning, he was so weak that, pull and tug as he did, the roller would not move.

Shen came up to her. "With Comrade Wong's permission, I will help Comrade Lee pull the roller."

"You cannot do both your work and his."

"Let me try."

"No," she said. "I will rake today."

At last, with September, the rain came. She heard it *tung tung* on the tin roof and then thunder down like horses on a gallop. It continued through the next day. They tried to work on the road but sank to their ankles in mud. Even the project leader saw it was useless and ordered them back to the barracks.

She was cleaning the mud off her shoes when she realized that the cloth covering the lining that Old Lee had made for her last winter was worn through to the paper core. She held the lining up to her small kerosene lamp. A single word of two characters showed through the hole—*gung luh*—highway. She smiled. Curious to know what the article, probably from an old newspaper, was saying about a highway and, hungry for something to read, anything, she stuck her index finger into the hole and pushed the cloth up a bit. "Make straight in the desert" . . . she pulled the cloth down . . . "a highway for our God."

Her heart froze. She took the tiny pair of scissors from the sewing kit she had been issued as a supervisor and clipped the stitches that bound the lining. Her hand was shaking so much that the task took twice as long as it should have. The cloth and paper were wet. She had to be very careful. But at last she could read the top layer of printing. "Comfort, comfort my people, says your God. Speak comfortably to Jerusalem, and cry unto her that her warfare is accomplished, that her iniquity is pardoned, for she has received of the Lord's hand double for all her sins. The voice of him that cries in the wilderness, Prepare the way of the Lord, make straight in the desert a highway for our God . . ."

She didn't know whether to laugh or be angry. All these months she had thought he was suffering for her, while all the time she had been unwittingly hiding pages from his Bible, walking on them every day. Suppose she had been caught? His punishment would be nothing compared to what she might receive. That pose of being an old fool, when all the time . . . Quickly she cut a patch from the seam of her jacket and mended the hole in the lining. No one must ever know.

When the sun came out at last, it was on a scene of devastation. The stretch of highway they had built so painstakingly over the last nine months had washed away. Most of the gravel had been swallowed up by a sea of mud. They must begin all over again.

Between the prolonged drought and the flood, the local crops were ruined. There was no harvest, and as the days grew colder, the weaker ones among them began to fall ill. Comrade Wong spent her days supervising a dwindling crew and her nights nursing the sick in the women's barracks.

One morning Old Lee did not appear. President Shen was pulling the roller and then going behind it to rake. She took the rake from his hands. He did not thank her but he did not object.

After a supper of thin gruel, she checked on the women who were sick. The flimsy barracks were as cold as the outdoors. She cautioned the women to sleep in all the clothes they owned and then went to her own shack to fall into exhausted sleep. *Ko-ko-ko* . . . *ko-ko-ko*. Was it a dream? She jumped up and opened the door. There stood the form of Old Lee, thin as a wraith, swaying in the doorway. He began to cough.

She pulled him in and shut the door. There was no kerosene for the lamp, so she lit her one candle. He bent over in a fit of coughing, beads of sweat gleaming on his forehead in the pale light. She grabbed the quilt off the cot, wrapped it around him, and eased him into the chair. "You shouldn't be walking about," she scolded. "You'll catch pneumonia."

He smiled through his coughing. "You are always so kind to me, sister."

She shook her head impatiently. "What are you doing out here in the middle of the night, comrade?"

"It is nearly Christmas," he said. "I wanted to give you a present."

"You gave me one last year," she said. "The linings for my shoes, remember?"

"But I never had a chance to tell you," he said. "The real present was not the linings, it was inside the linings."

"I—I found it," she said. Her face grew hot in the darkness. "I thought you might be using my shoes as your hiding place."

"No," he said. "I swear. It was for you. I can't read. I wanted you to have it in case we could not read together anymore. But there were too many pages. I could only put a little bit in for you."

"Forgive me," she said. She could not bear to look

at his sweating face, so thin and earnest. "You have been kinder to me than I to you."

"Oh, sister, you are always kind to me."

"My books." She choked out the words. "You are suffering because of me. It is not right. Tomorrow, I will explain—"

"No!" He dropped his voice. "You must never say a word. These hard times will pass, and then China will need you to teach again. I am only a night watchman." He reached out his hand. "Promise me this one thing before I die."

"You must not die. Not for me."

"We must all die, sister. I am well content. I go to be with Jesus. Just give me this one gift. Promise me you will not speak of this."

She could feel her heart swelling and aching inside her chest.

"Promise me?" he asked again. He wiped the sweat from his forehead with the back of his hand.

"Yes, yes, comrade. Now you must go. It isn't safe for you to be out in this cold."

THE NEXT DAY the whole project was ordered to remain in the dining hall after breakfast. Last night, the project leader informed them, Comrade Lee had been caught near the road. It was obvious that he meant to run away. "For his own good and the good of the group he must be punished."

Two of the supervisors stripped off the old man's jacket and began to beat him. Comrade Wong closed her eyes and put the back of her hand against her mouth to keep from screaming. She had promised him, she kept saying to herself. She had promised.

"Stop!" a voice cried. Comrade Wong opened her eyes. President Shen had covered Old Lee's back with his own body. "He was delirious last night. Can't you see? He's burning up with fever. Leave him alone!" But they pulled the president away and finished the beating.

She tried to speak to Shen later in the day, but each time he just looked at her tight-lipped, turned his back, and walked away. Finally she grabbed his arm. "You must tell me how he is!"

The president's eyes flashed. "He is dying. What did you expect?"

"Please. I beg you, bring him to my room tonight. I want to nurse him."

"You?"

"Please. I must do something."

"Aren't you afraid?" The tone was bitter.

"Yes," she said. "Of course I'm afraid. But it doesn't matter. Please bring him."

Late that night the two of them, Comrade Wong and the president, put Old Lee on her cot and covered him with all three of their quilts.

Even in his fever, he was smiling widely. "What friends God gives me," he said. "What friends."

"I have a present for you," she said. "I've taken the linings apart so I can read to you."

She brought her chair close to the cot.

"This is wonderful," the old man said. "I couldn't have dreamed of such a present." He motioned weakly for the president to sit down on the edge of the cot.

She began to read. " 'Comfort, comfort my people, says your God. Speak comfortably to Jerusalem . . .' "

"Ahh," the old man sighed. "I have never heard this part before."

" 'The voice of him that cries in the wilderness, Prepare the way of the Lord, make straight in the desert a highway for our God.' "

Old Lee struggled to sit up. "Do you hear? It is a word for us, here in this place. We are road builders."

"Oh, my elder brother, don't you see? It is you who have built the highway." She eased him down and covered him again. "Now, truly, you must rest."

"After I die I can rest," he said. "Please keep reading, sister."

But she was afraid that if she opened her mouth she would weep, so she handed the shoe-shaped page to the president and he leaned toward the flickering candle and continued:

" 'Every valley shall be exalted, and every mountain and hill shall be made low and the crooked shall be made straight, and the rough places plain;

" 'And the glory of the Lord shall be revealed, and all flesh shall see it together: for the mouth of the Lord has spoken it . . .' "

Star Lady

ON THE FIRST morning of her retirement, Rosamund McCormick got up at a quarter to seven. There was so much to do. She would begin with the house.

The real estate agent had warned her that December was a terrible month to sell a house. Even in a good year, people didn't buy in the winter, he had said. But Rosamund hadn't gotten to be one of the state's "Outstanding Women of Business" by listening to other people whine. There were plenty of wealthy young couples on the lookout for a beautifully kept ninety-year-old house with hand-carved mantelpieces and hardwood floors.

The neighborhood was no longer a handicap, she

told herself over coffee. There had been a time when her son had urged her to move. Many of the older houses had deteriorated, and nearly everyone she knew had fled to the suburbs. The patrons at Miller's grocery store had changed first in color and then in language, and, sad to say, there was usually a wino or two hanging about the small parking lot.

Grace Church, in which Rosamund had been baptized and married, had changed, too. When dear Dr. Lancaster died, they called a bearded boy right out of seminary who spoke to God as though He were a fraternity brother. The educational building, named the Weatherford-McCormick Building for her husband and her father, was turned into a day care center. And the choir— She shuddered. The choir loft that had once resounded with Bach oratorios now yipped with discordant modern jingles. She blanched to recall one awful one in which the refrain had been "Hooray for Jesus! He's our man!" Rosamund refused to make a fuss. She quietly moved her membership to the large downtown First Church, where the choir all had trained voices and the Trinity was addressed with proper deference.

During those years when the neighborhood as well

as the church and the corner grocery were going downhill, Rosamund had held on to her house. She had lived in it all her life, and she was simply too busy to take on the task of moving. Her husband, who had come into the family department store business when they married, died three years after her father, so Rosamund had to take over.

Now the neighborhood was on the verge of becoming fashionable once more. It was the perfect time to sell—a good time to leave. She had nothing to keep her. The business was in capable hands, her son was dead. She paused to refill her cup. Gail had remarried, of course, in less than two years. And, as if Rosamund hadn't suffered enough, the children, James's children, her grandchildren, had been adopted by Gail's new husband. She hardly saw them anymore.

She had planned to begin with the attic and work down through the house, throwing away everything except the antiques. She felt a great need to strip away all the physical encumbrances of her life and start afresh. But in the attic there were old letters and pictures, a worn-out football jersey, a weight-lifting set. No, it was not a day for the attic. Besides, from the window she could tell it was going to be one of those wonderful, almost springlike December days. She would begin with the garden. Hard physical exercise was the thing she needed.

The only time Rosamund ever allowed herself to wear trousers was in the garden. She used an old pair that had been her husband's, adding one of his hunting shirts for warmth. She tied her hair up in a scarf and put on her sturdy gardening shoes and yellow gloves.

She was pruning a rose bush when she spied the child staring at her through the hedge. Since she was on her knees, they were almost at eye level, except that it wasn't his eyes that she noticed first but the red, very runny nose. The hedge—she must make a note to call the nursery on Monday—was a bit scraggly at that spot, and the boy was standing in the alley behind it, obviously watching her.

"May I ask what you want?"

"Hi," he said, almost at the same moment.

"What are you doing there?" She couldn't help feeling that he had invaded her privacy, if not her territory, as he elbowed his way through the hedge.

"Watch that hedge!"

"Don't worry. It don't scratch much."

"I didn't think it would hurt *you*." But the boy, who seemed to be about eight, wasn't listening. He was taking her measure with his eyes, looking at her yellow gloves, her oversized pants, her worn shirt, even the threadbare canvas pad on which she was kneeling.

"Ain't got no coat, I bet," he said sympathetically.

"Of course I have a coat. I'm just not wearing it at the moment."

He nodded, a smile lighting up his dirt-smeared features. "Sure, lady," he said. "I understand."

"Understand? Understand what?"

"It's tough, being winter and all. But I want you to know you got friends in this world."

Rosamund was too startled to reply. Where had this creature come from? As if in answer, he nodded south. "They explained everything to us in Sunday school. People need to know that God loves them and that they got friends in the world."

"Well, that's very nice. Thank you very much," said Rosamund in her briskest voice, the one that sent the most persistent sales representatives backing out of a room. The boy didn't notice. "Well, good-bye," she said loudly, rising and pulling off her scarf. She would try to finish the roses at a better time.

"White hair," the boy said. "You really are old. Wow."

"I am sixty-five," Rosamund said tightly. "Not dead yet."

"Sixty-five." His eyes, a sort of grayish blue, widened. "My grandma is only fifty. You're old enough to be my great-grandma."

"Hardly. Don't you have a tissue or something for that nose?"

"No'm." He snuffled noisily.

For an awful moment she thought he was going to wipe his nose with his hand. She turned away. "Well, good-bye," she said and began to hurry toward the back steps. He came trotting after.

"We're supposed to come in and give you Christmas cheer."

"Thank you just the same. I'm quite cheerful enough already."

He snuffled once more. "But," he said, "if I don't pay you a visit, I don't get a star. See, the team that gets the most stars . . ."

What idiotic nonsense! Still what could you expect from a church that sang "Hooray for Jesus?" "Oh, all right." She was trapped and she knew it. "Come on in—for a minute. I'm busy."

He followed so closely up the back stairs that she was afraid he would trip on the heels of her shoes, but somehow they made it to the porch. "Wipe your feet on the mat, please," she said, demonstrating. He nodded vigorously, elaborately smearing the garden mud from one end of the mat to the other, losing a bit on the porch in his enthusiasm.

At the door, she slipped out of her garden shoes and was walking stocking-footed over to the kitchen closet when she realized he had taken off his sneakers and was tiptoeing after her in gray socks that she imagined she could smell across the room. Never mind. She'd feed him and dispense with him in ten minutes flat.

"I suppose you'll want something to eat," she said as she put on her house shoes and stowed the garden shoes in the closet.

"Oh, no," he said piously. "It's against the rules to take people's food."

"And I suppose it's also against the rules to blow your nose?"

"I don't think so," he said. "Preacher didn't mention nothing about it." The back of the hand from which the sneakers dangled headed toward the nose.

"Wait," she said, diving into her purse, which lay on the kitchen counter. "I may have a tissue." But she came up with a handkerchief of Belgian linen and lace that she had bought on her world tour two years before. It couldn't be helped. She handed the handkerchief to the boy.

He took it without thanks and blew his nose loudly and wiped it with all the ceremony he had expended on the doormat minutes before. Then he held it out to her.

"No, no," she said. "You keep it. You might need it later."

He nodded and stuffed it into his jeans pocket.

"Well—" How was she to get rid of him? "Thank you for your visit."

But he was just then settling himself on the kitchen stool. "I guess you're all alone in the world. Got no one to spend Christmas with or anything."

She opened her mouth, but before she could protest, he went on. "No kids. Not even a job, I bet."

"If you don't mind . . ."

"My mom's got a job. She puts the little ones in the center. Works out real good."

"That's nice," Rosamund said tightly.

"Yeah. I didn't know how lucky we were." He smiled sweetly at her. "I was just this grabby little kid, thinking about what I was going to get for Christmas. Stuff like that."

"I see. Well, it's been nice visiting with you, uh—"

"Buddy," he said. "Name's Buddy."

She might have guessed. "Thank you, Buddy. Now. I'm very busy. I'm going to be moving soon and I have a lot to do."

"Moving? They gonna make you move?"

"Buddy, really, I must—"

"But miz—miz—that's terrible."

"Not your worry." She wasn't about to give the child her name or any more of her time. She swept him out the door, handing him his sneakers on the porch. He didn't seem offended and called out cheery greetings as he went, reminding her more than once that God loved her and that she was no longer friendless. She smiled back primly, but the minute he was gone, she collapsed against the door, laughing until the tears rolled down her cheeks. She had to go poking about in her handbag for a tissue, which made her start laughing all over again.

She made a conscious effort to pull herself together. She was not going to become one of those old women who talk to themselves or laugh out loud in empty houses. But at the moment she couldn't think of anyone to call and tell. Her friends wouldn't be able to imagine how very comical it was—that solemn little runny-nosed boy bringing her Christmas cheer so his Sunday school team could get a star. And she had given him her Belgian linen handkerchief . . . James would have loved it. But James was dead and she hardly ever saw his wife or children anymore.

The laughter evaporated as she thought of her grandchildren, who were growing up without her. She had tried to visit, but Gail and she had never been close, and Gail's new husband seemed ill at ease in her presence. James's children, who had once been so tiny and dear, had suddenly become loud and unmannerly, eager to be off to some party or other. She had begun spending all her holidays in Florida. It was easier on everyone.

A FEW DAYS later, there was a note on her door when she got back from the hairdresser's. It was on lined notebook paper and clumsily decorated with crayoned stars and Christmas trees.

Dear friend (she could barely decipher the handwriting), this is to invite you to our Christmas Joy Service on Christmas Eve at 7 p.m. at

Grace Church. We want you to know that God loves you and you have lots of friends. There will be eats, too.

Your special friend,
Buddy Collins

P.S. Don't worry. You can wear your old clothes. It don't matter.

Christmas at Grace Church. She remembered all too well the last Christmas Eve service she had attended in Grace Church. There were at least eight different-colored electric flames in the windows. The minister paraded two dozen or more squawky-voiced little children to the front to sing some jangly tune . . . with rhythm instruments. Rosamund sighed. Tacky. That was the only word for it.

She allowed herself, just for a moment, to go back to the Christmas Eves years ago when the sanctuary had been dimly lit with a pair of standing candelabra among the poinsettias. Into the darkness and the hush, the choir, sounding like a single voice from the vestibule, began the ancient carol "Let all mortal flesh keep silence . . ." Then they walked in solemn procession down the main aisle, carrying candles, the haunting melody growing in power as they came, until at last they massed under the majestic pipes of the choir loft ablaze with light. The music soared, filling the church and reverberating from the great dark beams of the rafters:

"Alleluia, Alleluia, Alleluia, Lord most High!"

She shivered at the memory of it. The wonder and the power and the mystery. And now . . .

She balled up the grubby little note and dropped it into the hall basket.

But Buddy, as she found, was not to be dismissed so easily. Two days before Christmas, she was in the midst of decorating her tree when the doorbell rang.

"Hi," he said cheerfully.

"Oh, Buddy, I'm very busy right now. I'm decorating my Christmas tree."

"You got a tree?" He rushed by her at the door to come in for a look. "Oh." He sounded relieved. "It's real tiny." He went closer to the table on which the tree stood. "Not even real." This time his voice segued into its sorrowful key. "But it's nice." He looked up, his dirty little face radiating sincerity.

"Thank you, Buddy."

"It's real nice you keep trying. Some old people just give up."

"Do they, now."

"Yeah. You ought to see the ones over to the home. It's real pitiful—some of 'um don't even know who they are anymore."

"You'll be glad to know that I still know who I am."

"Good for you." He beamed, patting her arm. "You just keep it up." He picked up a glass ball from the box on the table and shook it.

"Buddy," she said as quietly as possible, "that ornament is nearly one hundred years old. Would you be kind enough to put that back into the box? Very carefully."

"Huh? Oh, sure." She watched, hardly breathing, as his hand, which was too big for his small body, lurched against the side of the box, rattling the delicately painted glass ball back into its place.

"Cost too much to get new ones these days, don't it?"

"Yes," she said, sighing with relief. "Well, Buddy, it was nice of you to come, but I am busy right now."

"I could help decorate your tree."

"No!" The word came out more sharply than she'd intended. "It's just that I'm getting ready to move and . . ."

"Oh, yeah." Sympathy poured through the dirt on

his face. "Oh, yeah. I almost forgot." He started backing toward the front door. "But don't you worry. Just remember—God loves you, and you got friends in this world."

"I won't forget, Buddy. Be sure your team gets another star."

He missed the irony, of course, beaming his most evangelical smile. That's who he reminded her of. Those television evangelists with their toothy smiles. Only their faces were cleaner.

SHE FORGOT ABOUT her little gospel bearer until the phone call early Christmas Eve morning.

"Rosamund? Merry Christmas! It's me, Gail."

"Yes, Gail." She could feel her body stiffening.

"It's been too long since we've seen you."

"Yes, well, I've been quite busy."

"We'd love to have you join us for dinner tomorrow."

"I have plans."

"I would have called you earlier, but I just assumed you'd be in Florida as usual."

"No. I'm moving down as soon as I sell the house. I felt the need to stay and get it ready."

Why was Gail laughing? Rosamund hadn't said anything funny. She'd never understood Gail. She felt the impulse to slam down the receiver but restrained herself. "Thank you for calling," she said crisply.

"No, no, no, wait—" Gail was trying to suppress her giggles. "I have to explain."

"Yes?" She was curious despite her annoyance.

"Peter called." Gail could only mean Peter Freedman, the new president of Weatherford Department Store, Inc. "Someone called the office to ask about you."

"About me?"

"Yes, apparently"—and here another giggle bubbled up—"apparently there is a rumor going around the neighborhood that you have lost all your money and are on the verge of eviction."

"Eviction?"

"I know it's crazy, but that's what the minister told Peter."

"What minister?" But she knew the answer. "That bearded boy at Grace Church?"

"That's the one."

"Buddy." Rosamund bit the name as though it were a profanity.

"Pardon?"

"I've got something I have to attend to, Gail. I'll talk to you later."

"About dinner. . ."

"Later." She clanged down the phone. That dirty-faced, runny-nosed busybody, making a fool of her at the church, at the company, even with Gail. Just because she'd tried to be nice.

She had a cup of tea to calm herself before calling the church office.

"Grace Church. God loves you, and you have friends in the world. Merry Christmas!"

"Yes. This is Rosamund Weatherford McCormick. I would like to speak to the pastor."

"He's not in right now. Can I take a message?"

She was delighted to note that all the bounce had seeped out of the secretary's voice. "In that case," she continued, carving each word out of ice, "I would like the telephone number of a child by the name of Buddy Collins. I understand he attends your Sunday school."

"Uh, Mrs. McCormick. Maybe you ought to speak to Bill first."

"Bill?"

"Reverend Farley."

"I thought you just said he wasn't in."

"He's not, but—"

"Then I will take the Collins's number."

"I think Reverend Farley wants to talk to you about a misunderstanding."

"The telephone number, if you please."

"I don't know if they have a phone. I don't seem to have a listing. . ."

She finally extracted the street address from the reluctant secretary. It was one of the tumbledown houses that backed hers on the alley. She went to her bedroom, carefully applied her makeup, and dressed in a soft wool peacock-blue dress, and—although it was totally inappropriate for morning wear—pinned a large diamond brooch at her throat. Then she put on her cashmere overcoat. If Buddy had difficulty identifying quality, his mother ought to be able to recognize that Buddy's Sunday school project was not teetering over the edge of either senility or poverty.

She stormed down the alley, around the corner, and up the street, looking for the proper number. She guessed the house before she got to it—one of the once handsome Victorian mansions that had been chopped into apartments. The grassless front yard was overrun with small children and dogs, all of which seemed to be wagging their tongues at her. In a tangle of frantic barks and high-pitched squeals—"Whatcha want, lady?

Whatcha want?"—she made her way through the yard to the front door. There was no bell, so she knocked loudly, nearly bruising her knuckles in the effort to make herself heard over the din.

At last someone came to the door. Buddy, carrying a baby almost as large and runny-nosed as himself.

"Oh." He cocked his head. "My mom's at work." And then suddenly, as though finally recognizing her above the cashmere collar and taking in the meaning of her visit, he hung his head. "Preacher told me you ain't being thrown out of your house."

"No," she said, her anger already evaporated.

"I ain't going to bother you anymore. Don't worry." He began to close the door with his foot, juggling the baby as he did so.

Just then a little girl who had been in the yard bumped past her and shoved the door wide open. "This your star lady, Buddy? The one you was telling about?"

"Shut up!"

"Is it? Is it?" She danced around, looking at Rosamund from every possible angle.

"No!" Buddy yelled. "You don't get no stars for bothering rich people. You just get stars for helping the poor and needy."

"You didn't get a star for me?" Rosamund asked.

"I got the wrong house," he said. "Supposed to see this old lady on welfare, and I got the wrong house. Preacher give me the devil for it, too."

Rosamund smiled despite herself. "We're going to get your star back," she said.

The boy sneaked a look and when he saw the smile, he smiled shyly back, shifting the squirming baby to his other hip.

"I don't care," he said. "It was dumb, anyway."

"But the preacher ought to know."

"Know what?" He snuffled.

"That . . . sometimes . . . rich old ladies need friends, too."

"Yeah?" He jiggled the baby to quiet it, his eyes on its almost hairless head. "Wanna come to church with me tonight?" he whispered.

"Of course," she said.

THE SANCTUARY WAS lit with the same garish electric candles, and the music, if anything, was worse than she had remembered. The congregation was a variegated mix of race and age.

In a specially designated front section, all the children in Buddy's Sunday school class were sitting with their star people. The children's beaming faces alternated with the tired faces of the neighborhood's aged outcasts. Rosamund was sure that the man two down from her was one of Miller's grocery store's winos, his breath coming down the pew sour and strong. On the other side of Buddy, a little girl, pink ribbons bouncing in her black plaits, was proudly arranging the crutches of her star lady under the pew in front.

Instead of the stately alleluias of bygone years, Rosamund could hear the cry of a sleepy baby in the rear, echoed by the hacking cough of an old man at the end of her row.

After an exuberant attack on "Hark! The Herald Angels Sing" that would have roused the dead to protest, the bearded young preacher read the Christmas story in a jarring modern version. "What is the message of Christmas?" he asked. "What does it mean to us that this baby was born in a barn all those years ago? Today, in Grace Church, when we hear this story, what does it make us want to say to our neighbors?"

"God loves you!" the children yelled. "And you got friends in the world!"

Buddy turned to her and smiled. His face, cleaner than she had ever seen it, reflected all the light in the sanctuary. "Me, too," he whispered hoarsely, patting her knee. "I got me a friend, too."

Tears started in her eyes. Suddenly she found herself snuffling. She began to poke into her purse but, before she could find a tissue, Buddy jabbed her arm. He was returning her handkerchief—clean, slightly gray, and very wrinkled, but obviously scrubbed.

She mouthed a thank-you and gently blew her nose. What would James have thought—Rosamund the star lady, sitting in the second pew with all the poor and needy of the neighborhood, blowing her nose. Or Gail? And the children? She couldn't wait to tell them tomorrow when she saw them.

A slightly different version of this story was published in The Virginian-Pilot, *December 24, 1982.*

Amazing Grace

HE KNEW THEY were lost. But he would not allow himself to think what that might mean. The freezing rain *rat-tat-tat*ted on the narrow blacktop. They must be somewhere in the Appalachian foothills west of Marion. He should turn left at the next major crossroads to get back toward 81—shouldn't he? Why were there no signs?

It must have been an hour since he turned off the highway to look for a gas station that was open. But after nine o'clock on Christmas Eve in the middle of nowhere, of course, there was none.

He glanced over at Margaret. Thank God she was asleep. He could imagine what she would be saying if she weren't. No matter how hard he tried, there was always something for Margaret to sneer at. He could remember—it seemed a lifetime ago—he could remember a time when the sight of her asleep had made his whole body stir with tenderness. But now—her mouth slightly open, her head bobbing with the motion of the car, the seatbelt barely stretching around her great swollen stomach—how she would despise being regarded as ridiculous. But there she was: beautiful, clever Margaret, looking nearly ugly and very stupid.

He turned his mind back to the road ahead. The headlights, slashed by the sparkling rain, made a short path of light in an ocean of blackness.

It was her fault. They had never spent Christmas in Bristol before, but this year, with the peculiar willfulness that had characterized her pregnancy, she had determined that they must go home for Christmas. It was as though they had already agreed, though neither of them had said so, that the apartment on Sixteenth Street was no longer home.

He had been all set to have it out with her last spring. He was so tired—tired of all the traps life laid out for him: the job; the bills that went on and on for things he no longer wanted; the clever, brittle people they called friends. He had made up his mind to tell her that she must let him go before he suffocated. Where he went didn't matter, just somewhere away. But before he could say anything, she told him about the baby, and he was trapped again.

"Oh, hell!" He wrenched the car back off the shoulder.

She jolted awake. "Where are we?"

"How should I know?"

"Paul—we're not on 81." It was an accusation.

He sighed rather than try to reply.

"Paul!" Her voice thinned into the familiar whine. Oh, God, don't let her start picking me apart, not now.

"It's all right," he said roughly. "I'm looking for a gas station. Just go on back to sleep."

She leaned against the seat, but he knew her eyes were wide open. For a few minutes they drove on, listening to the hum of the motor and the tattoo of the icy rain.

"You're lost, aren't you?" How like her to say "You're lost," not "We're lost." The car began to sputter and slow. He pulled off the road just as it stopped dead.

"Not only lost," he said, turning to look full upon her white, puffy face, "but out of gas." He leaned his head against his hands on the wheel. Now what? He sighed deeply.

"What are you going to do? We can't stay here."

As she spoke, the thought occurred to him that that would be the only sensible thing to do—wait in the car until morning. But like most of his ideas, they were vetoed before he even had a chance to voice them. He started to get out of the car.

"Where are you going?"

"Margaret, you just said we couldn't stay here. I'm going to look for help."

"You're not going to leave me alone!"

"Margaret, the weather is terrible. Just stay here—try to sleep. I'll get your heavy coat from the back . . ."

"Paul—you can't. Please don't leave me." He gave in, as he always did, and helped her out of the car onto the road. Then he reached into the driver's side, shut off the lights, and slammed the door.

The darkness was absolute. He had never experienced total blackness before. It was terrifying not to be able to see anything. He waited for Margaret to make a crack about the flashlight that wasn't in the car-door pocket, but she stood silent, close enough to him so that he could feel her trembling.

Only the slippery blacktop under their feet told him that they were still on the road. The wind and rain went through his body like jagged knives, and his right arm and shoulder ached from the weight of her body as she leaned into him. He couldn't tell how far they had walked. The blackness robbed him of any perception of time or distance. But as they went on, he could feel her faltering. If only she had been willing to stay in the car. She felt like a drowning swimmer, who would pull and pull until she dragged them both under forever into the black, black nothingness.

Just when he thought his heart and lungs would burst, they turned a curve in the road, and suddenly, up to his left, he saw a light. He nearly dragged her as he climbed toward it, brambles and weeds tearing away at their legs.

The light was from the window of a small cabin. It was scarcely more than a shack, but to Paul it was light and shelter. He banged on the door so loudly that the whole framework shook. There was no answer. This time he beat with both fists and yelled, but there was still no reply.

He tried the latch. It fell open. "Come in, Goldilocks," he said, and Margaret made a sound almost like a laugh.

A kerosene lamp sat on a table by the front window, barely lighting the tiny room. He picked it up and went slowly, ducking under the low lintel into the back room of the cabin. The room was filled with a bed, but there was no one in it.

"Margaret," he called, "come in here and lie down. I'll make a fire, and then we can decide what to do next."

She didn't answer, and when he came back into the front room, he found her in an ancient rocker, doubled over in pain.

"Oh, Lord," he said. "No."

"Oh, Paul, I'm such a fool."

He put the lamp down and then ran his hands through his wet hair and over his mouth. "Well," he said. "Well—"

"I'll go lie down," she said. "It takes a long time. The first one always does."

He made a fire in the Franklin stove, and because he had never done so, it sputtered and died three or four times before any of the larger wood caught the flame.

Then he went to the bedroom door and leaned under the lintel. "I'm going to find help—if you think there's time—otherwise . . ."

"Don't . . . ," she stopped. "No, you're right. We need help. I'll manage."

He cleared his throat. "I wouldn't choose to leave you here alone."

"I know. Thanks."

He found another lantern, and the pale light was so comforting that the wind and cold seemed less hostile. He walked rapidly down the road, keeping his senses alert for any sign of life. It was not long before he saw light ahead and heard, as he approached, what seemed to be the sound of a running stream. As he drew closer, the sound turned out to be voices.

But the quality of the voices was strange to him; perhaps they were foreigners. It was not the rhythm of conversation as he recognized it.

The building was larger than the cabin and lighted by electricity. The door was cracked open. Now the voices reminded him of instruments tuning up before a concert. He raised his hand to knock, thought better of it, and gently pushed the door open.

He stepped inside, but he couldn't adjust himself at once. It was like coming out into bright sunlight after a matinee. People were milling about the room—all speaking—but not to one another. He couldn't sort out any words until he heard a harsh masculine voice say quite distinctly:

"Amazing grace! Ohhh, amazing grace!"

He turned toward the voice and to his utter astonishment discovered that it came from a tiny, bent woman—so old that the skin stretched tight across her face and dropped to hang loosely below her chin.

She raised her head at an angle to look him straight in the eyes. "Ohhh, sinner! The amazing grace!"

He came to his senses then. "I need help," he said, raising his voice over the cacophonous background. She looked at him blankly. "I need help, a doctor." He grasped her thin arm, but she shook it free in an impatient gesture and moved away.

"There ain't no doctor here, son." The speaker had a florid, kindly face above a large flowery housedress.

"Can *you* help me? I've left my wife in a cabin down the road. She's in labor, I think."

The woman was already putting on a green cloth coat. "Kerosene lamp in the window?" He nodded.

"Granny!"

"Amazing grace!"

"Granny, this boy's wife's down at your place, 'bout to give birth. Get your coat and let's go." The old woman's eyes came into focus for a moment and a strange expression came over her face.

"Hurry, Granny."

The woman, who told him her name was Ada Bowman, herded them to the door. There she produced from somewhere under her coat the largest flashlight Paul had ever seen. The sight of it filled Paul with hope. Here was a kind woman, a sensible woman, an angel of light armed against the darkness and ignorance of the world.

They walked back to the cabin in a great beam of light. Mrs. Bowman chattered brightly as they went. "Granny, you leave that kerosene lamp burning and you gonna come home from church some night to a pile o' ashes." Then in a confidential tone—"She don't believe in electricity. You know how old folks are."

But Paul didn't know about old folks like Granny, who was trotting along just a few steps behind the fast pace that he and Mrs. Bowman were setting. She groaned in her strange voice, "Lord, I thank thee!" and "Oh, Lord, you have heard my prayer!"

"She's got so she don't know where she's at half the time—but she's a good old soul."

"Lord, you have given me a precious sign."

"She's—she's in the other room," he told Mrs. Bowman as they reached the cabin, his fears flooding back.

"Aw right, aw right, son," said Mrs. Bowman soothingly. "We take care of everything here. I guess I've delivered forty babies in my time. You just help Granny get the place warm"—the feeble fire had gone out, of course—"and then there ain't nothing to do but wait."

HE MUST HAVE fallen asleep in the rocker. His eyes went to the closed bedroom door. How could he sleep when Margaret . . . ?

"Lord, I asked you for a sign, and it has been given unto me. Praise the Lord, you His angels! You mighty ones who do His will!"

The old woman was sitting on a low stool before the stove, her body rocking back and forth in a kind of trance. The firelight gave her transparent skin a strange glow.

"Oh, Lord, my house is poor and lowly, but you have visited me with your salvation."

He listened to the harsh voice without comprehension. It seemed to tear out of the frail body as though it was encased there against its will. The old eyes were closed. She was oblivious to his staring.

"Lord, now lettest thy servant depart in peace, according to thy word. For mine eyes have seen thy salvation . . ."

He got up. He wished there was some way of quieting the woman. She was getting on his nerves, and if Margaret could hear her . . .

He went to the closed door. "Mrs. Bowman, I'm going down to the car for a minute and get some things, okay?"

"Fine. Fine."

He had gotten as far as the door and picked up Mrs. Bowman's great flashlight, when, without warning, the old woman spun about on her stool and cried out:

"Joseph, thou son of David!"

A chill went through Paul's body.

She rose to her feet, her small bright eyes fixed on his face.

"Joseph, thou son of David. Fear not!" She flung out a bony arm. "Fear not! The Lord is with thee!"

He stared a moment, his mouth open, but no words came. The cabin seemed suffocating. "I've got to go," he said at last, "to the car—to get uh—uh" and left her standing there, her arm still stretched out in the gesture of an avenging angel.

He ran down the path to the road, the giant flashlight throwing a crazy beam before him. When he got to the roadway, he forced himself to walk. Senility did weird things to people. Poor old woman. He tried to laugh, but it came out pinched and unnatural on the silent night air. Poor, crazy old woman. The bearers of her sign from heaven didn't even believe in God. Joseph, son of David, indeed. Well, at least he was as worthy of his title as Margaret was of hers. The Holy Mother. He could hear her high-pitched laughter as she repeated the words. But even as he smiled at the thought, something icy grew inside his chest.

"Fear not!"

What did the old woman think he was afraid of? Or was that part of the other story? The one she had plunged him into against his will? Of course he had been afraid earlier. Anyone would have been— Margaret going into labor in this godforsaken place, the car out of gas, not knowing where they were, the blackness. That was the worst of it—the utter dark into which they moved like the yawning mouth of nothingness swallowing them up.

He was shivering. Lord, it was cold. The beam

caught the shape of the car ahead. He ran toward it, unlocked the door, and slid under the wheel. He'd rest, just for a minute, before starting back. It was a long way. He hadn't just imagined it in the dark.

"Fear not."

But now everything was going to be all right. Mrs. Bowman had said so. Why was his heart still thudding against his chest? Oh, Lord, Lord, he *was* afraid. What he had mistaken for weariness was fear. He was afraid of caustic Margaret, who could destroy him with a word or just the expression on her face. He was afraid of failing and of the boss who watched him, just waiting for it to happen, knowing that sooner or later . . .

He was afraid of going out of his Washington apartment at night. He was afraid of speaking to people at those noisy, cruel parties. He was afraid of a world that went on day after weary day as though nothing would ever change, and then suddenly, in a stroke as capricious as it was evil, would come the firing of an assassin's bullet or some other monstrous, unimaginable evil that would make nothing ever be the same. But afterward life would ease back into the same gray weariness, the residue of catastrophe simply adding a bit more fear to the burden of one's soul.

"Fear not. The Lord is with thee." And who knew,

perhaps God himself was nothing more than a yawning chasm of darkness, ready to swallow . . .

He pulled himself together. He must be a man, at least. Had Margaret cried out? Margaret, who never had a tooth filled without novocaine. Margaret, without a wrinkle in her clothes or a hair out of place.

"I'll manage." That's what she said. "I'll manage." He got her suitcase from the trunk.

There was still no moon, but a dozen stars had pricked their way through the darkness. He stood still, looking up, took several deep breaths, and began to walk back.

"It's a fine boy." Mrs. Bowman was at the stove, one hand on her ample hip and the other lifting a cup to her lips. "Coffee?" He shook his head. The old woman lay back in the rocker. She seemed to be asleep.

"My—my wife?"

"God bless her. What a little soldier she is! Go on in. She's got something to show off to you."

"Paul?"

He was afraid to go in, but he made himself stoop down and enter. In the flickering light he could see them, Margaret cradling a tiny, red-faced creature on her arm.

"Isn't he beautiful?" There was a new tone in her

voice—a wonder—a radiance that he had never heard before.

"You were great, Margaret." His voice broke. "Lord knows I wouldn't have planned it this way."

"It's okay," she said softly. "You found Mrs. Bowman for me. Everything's all right." She motioned him to a place on the bed, and when he sat down, she continued softly, "Everything's all right. Don't worry, love."

"For unto us a child is born, unto us a son is given . . ."

The old woman stood in the doorway, her rasping voice crying out the familiar words.

"Oh, Lord, we praise thee for this precious sign . . ."

"It's all right, love," she whispered. "She's harmless. It's just that she's got the idea— Well, it's Christmas and she's got the idea that our baby is some sort of miracle."

"Perhaps he is," he said softly.

"Amazing grace!" It was a shout of joy. "Ohhh, Lord! What amazing grace!"

Exultate Jubilate

CHRISTMAS IS OVER. Sally is putting the children to bed, and I am sitting in the living room staring at a rocking horse and trying to figure out what happened to me last night. You must understand, first of all, that I have always entertained a certain sympathy for Scrooge. There he was, going about his business as best he knew how while all around him the world was going mad. 'Tis the season to be jolly? Come, now. What is there to be jolly or merry or even mildly happy about? How can anyone who watches the evening news on a daily basis work up a case of holiday cheer? Frankly, I weary of Christmas carols that start jangling through the malls on Halloween. The decorations on the lampposts that the city fathers drag out every Friday after Thanksgiving have begun to show their age. And so have I.

My wife is another story. She goes into a frenzy of decorating and baking and, since August, has been in a panic trying to decide whether or not to give a present to the Steadmans. I just try to stay out of her way.

I want my kids to be happy, but it's hard to be patient when they pester me for months for junk they've seen advertised on TV that anyone over ten knows wouldn't last out the twelve days of Christmas. Can someone explain to me why, as the days grow shorter, the pitch of children's voices gets higher and higher? Besides, this year business has been, if not bad, certainly not robust, and I simply didn't have the money, not to mention energy and goodwill, to waste on the latest fad.

Still, the only reason I didn't go around literally grunting "Bah! Humbug!" this year was because of the kids. They are only three and six, and I am enough of a hypocrite not to try to ruin their excitement, much as my head aches to tone down the shrill. But somehow I drew the line at going to the Christmas Eve service last night. Once I slid out from under my mother's "Thou shalt nots," I became quite happily an Easter,

Christmas, and whenever-my-mother-was-visiting Christian. But this year even Christmas seemed too much.

I told my wife I would stay behind to organize the stocking gifts and put the rocking horse together. Every year it's two or three in the morning before we can get to bed. And then we're too angry with each other to sleep. The year of Mike's tricycle was a low point in Christmases past—one reason Jenny was getting a rocking horse.

"The children will be so disappointed if you don't come," she said.

"Oh, they don't really expect me to go to church."

"But it's snowing, and you know how I hate to drive in the snow."

"Why is it that I have three more years of payments on a certain four-wheel-drive Subaru Wagon?"

"But I don't like leaving you here all by yourself on Christmas Eve," she said. "You'll get gloomy and moody."

"In two hours," I whispered, lest any little ears be nearby, "I'll have that rocking horse put together, and all we'll have to do is stuff the stockings and dream of sugarplums." That cinched it. She remembered all too well the long night of the tricycle.

"Daddy isn't feeling up to church tonight," she told the children. I coughed obligingly and helped her zipper the snowsuits and yank on the boots, and happily waved them off to church.

A half hour later, I was not so happy. The rocking horse that I had so carefully purchased was proving to be, in my mother's picturesque phrase, "an instrument of the devil."

It was not on rockers, but attached to its stand by huge, coiled springs. I had, by the hardest effort, pulled three of the four springs and hooked them into the stand. But every time I got the fourth nearly in place —sweating and straining to make it stretch to the last eye—the spring would recoil viciously, gouging my flesh as it flew through my hand.

I was glumly staring into the living room fireplace with a large brandy in my hand when the doorbell rang. My impulse was to ignore it. Sally had the garage opener. She wouldn't be ringing the front doorbell, and nobody we knew would be dropping in for a visit. The bell rang twice before I roused myself, put down my drink, and shuffled to the door.

Through the peephole I could see a youngish-looking man. He was wearing a windbreaker, but his head and hands were bare. He was carrying a paste-board box and he looked frozen.

I opened the door about an inch. "Yes?"

He smiled. His lips were cracked and his nose and cheeks raw. "Would you like to buy some Christmas greens?"

The man had obviously not seen the inside of our house. "Sorry," I said, starting to close the door on his smile.

"Well, merry Christmas to you," he was saying when I remembered the stupid horse. Maybe the guy could help.

I opened the door wide. "Come in," I said with heartiness so false any fool would have suspected me of being up to no good. "Come in and get warm, at least. You must be frozen."

He put down his box of greens, stamped the snow off his thin shoes, and stepped in gratefully. "Not many sales tonight," he said. "I expect most people are all ready for Christmas."

"Yeah," I said. "Could I get you something hot? I think there's still some coffee."

"Gee," he said. "That's real nice of you." He followed me down the greenery-festooned hall to the kitchen. "Wow," he said, "you sure don't need more greens. You're loaded."

"My wife's a little bit crazy on the subject of Christmas," I said, pouring out a mug of coffee for each of us. "Milk and sugar?"

"If it's no trouble." He held the mug out for me to put in the milk and then the sugar, and then stick in a spoon. "Thank you," he said, stirring deliberately while he looked around our big kitchen. Sally had wreaths and ribbons even in there. His hands were so chapped they looked as though they'd been bleeding.

"Smells like Christmas," he said.

I hadn't noticed, but in addition to the evergreens the room was full of the warm odor of cinnamon and cloves and the Christmas bread that Sally had baked that afternoon.

"Nice, isn't it?" he said.

"Well, yes, I suppose so. If you like that sort of thing." My mind was on getting the horse done before Sally and the children got back, but I couldn't very well snatch the coffee I'd just given him from his hands.

"I guess you have a pretty tree, too."

Well, what could I do? He obviously wanted to see our tree. I led him back down the hall to the living room. Our house is not one of these energy-efficient moderns. It's Victorian with a fifteen-foot ceiling, and the tree scraped it. I think Sally picked out the house so she could have monster Christmas trees. There is certainly no other reason for a ceiling of that height. You should see our heating bill.

The visitor was standing there, his mouth open, his eyes shining like a three-year-old's. "That's the most beautiful tree I ever saw in my life," he whispered.

"Yes, well," I felt almost apologetic. "My wife——"

He turned, his face still full of awe. "She must be a wonderful person."

"As wives go . . ." I tried to joke, but it wasn't going to work. The guy was as sincere as a cocker spaniel. "Don't let your coffee get cold," I said.

He ducked his head and took a sip, but over the rim he was eyeing my sound system. Oh, dear. Maybe he was casing the joint. I took his elbow to steer him to the family room, where one three-legged rocking horse sat waiting, but he resisted me.

"I know I shouldn't ask you . . ." He smiled his childlike smile. It was impossible to believe that such a lovely smile, cracked lips and all, belonged to a potential thief. "I mean, you've been so nice, but I'm so hungry for real music. Just while I'm drinking your good coffee?"

He looked hungry for meat and potatoes, but how could I refuse such a request? "Okay," I said, "a bargain. You can choose any music in the cabinet if you'll help me put together a rocking horse for my daughter."

His smile broke into a laugh. "I'm getting the best end of that." He handed me his still almost-full cup and fairly ran to the cabinet.

While he fingered the CDs and tapes lovingly, I wondered what he might choose. There wasn't much there that would appeal to a person of his class. There were dozens of recordings of Christmas carols—even one, so help me, of those cartoon chipmunks singing traditional tunes.

"Here," he said, his eyes glowing. "This one, please."

"Are you sure?" He had handed me Mozart. The Colin Davis London Symphony recording of Mozart's sacred music. Now wouldn't you have been surprised?

"Do you mind?" he asked anxiously when he saw my hesitation.

"No, of course not," I said.

"I don't look like a Mozart lover, right?" His smile was on crooked now.

"Well, I mean . . ." There was no way of getting

out of that one. I put down the coffee cups and inserted the tape.

I waited for the great "Kyrie in D Minor" to boom out, and after adjusting the sound slightly, picked up the coffee cups and started for the family room and the horse.

"No!" He grabbed my wrist. Coffee sloshed into the saucers from both cups. "Listen."

"Kyrie Eleison!" the voices demanded. *Lord have mercy!* "Christe Eleison!" *Christ have mercy!* I thought I had heard it before, but I realized, as I looked at my visitor, that I had never really heard it. His eyes were closed. I felt distinctly uncomfortable. "Come on," I said, slipping my wrist out from under his hand, being careful to keep from spilling coffee on Sally's rug. "We've got to get that fool horse done before my family gets home."

He opened his eyes and looked at me. I thought he was going to object, but he grinned. "Yes," he said, "our bargain."

"It's in there, too." I jerked my head at the sound system. "The music goes all over the house."

"Oh," he breathed. "That's wonderful. You can live in music." He followed me to the den.

There sat, or should I say, sagged the horse with Mozart showering down upon its head. "If you pull that spring," I said, nodding at it with my head, "I'll try to yank this side in toward you so you can hook it."

He was listening to the Kyrie and not to me. I hated to interrupt him, but we did have this bargain. "The horse," I said with a bit more urgency in my voice. "They're likely to get home any minute . . ."

He nodded, but I knew he wasn't paying attention to me. I should have been angry, but somehow, he was forcing me to listen to the music, too. I handed him back his coffee. "Just through the Kyrie, all right?" I said. "Then we do the horse." I'm not sure if he heard, but he took the coffee and sat cross-legged on the floor, his head cocked toward the wall-mounted speaker.

I sat on the couch, watching him listen, but it was not a stranger's profile I was seeing but the face of my father singing this very Mozart one Christmastime when the civic chorus had decided against the usual *Messiah*. My father died when I was seventeen, so I must have been a young teenager.

I loved to watch my father sing. Of all the faces in the chorus, his was the one that appeared to be listening rather than showing off. He always seemed to believe the music that he sang. And although I was an arrogant kid full of questions and resisting any answers, I loved the humble reverence I saw in him. I never told him though. It wouldn't have been cool or neat or whatever our catchphrase was in those days. And then he died.

I went to the kitchen and cut a piece of Sally's Christmas bread and brought it to the stranger—to make up for never having told my father that I loved to watch him sing. "You're too kind," the young man murmured. Me, too kind? Lord have mercy, indeed.

How, I wondered, in some future Christmas would my children remember me? Certainly not as I remembered my father—his face glowing with the glory of the music he sang.

I could almost see a huge festive table with a grown-up Mike and Jenny and their families gathered around. And Sally, white and wrinkled, but still not a bad-looking woman. "I wish your father could be here today," she was saying.

"Dad?" Mike was frowning. "He'd hate it. I mean, the very fact that we are here would mean that civilization hadn't blown itself to bits. You know how he hated to be proved wrong about anything."

"Mike! What a thing to say!" Thatta girl, Sally.

"You remember the news bulletins?" Mike went on.

"Children"—now Jenny, my sweet little girl, has jumped into it—"children, the minute the tree went up your grandfather would begin reading aloud items from the newspaper to prove how awful the world was—that there was no peace, no goodwill, no hope, no joy—"

"Exultate Jubilate!" the choir sang out. With a chill of relief, I shook off the ghost of Christmas-yet-to-come and turned my attention again to my visitor. His face shone as his cracked lips moved, mouthing the Latin words of joy and exaltation. How could he, with raw face and chapped and bleeding hands, be joyful? How, in fact, could the starving Mozart have known such a moment of exquisite joy? How could a baby born in a barn bring such beauty, such glory into this greedy, self-destructive, cruel world?

Suddenly I heard the clatter of the garage door. I jumped from the couch. "They're back!"

"Oh." The young man hastily picked the crumbs of bread off his windbreaker and jeans and popped them into his mouth. He half rose. "I'm sorry," he said. "I was lost . . ."

"It's too late. I'll get them into the front room. You

just slip out when you can, and make sure the door is shut." He looked puzzled, maybe a little hurt. "The horse," I explained. "I don't want the children to see it." And I slammed the family room door on his confused and embarrassed face.

"What glorious music!" Sally said as I met them in the back hall. "It makes me feel like being jubilant." She's a beautiful woman, especially when she's happy. "I'm glad you've been listening to Mozart," she continued, taking off her hat and shaking out her lovely hair. "I rather pictured a different scenario. . ." She gave me a wry look.

"Okay," I said to the children. "Let's take all the boots and snowsuits off in the back hall."

"It's cold out here, Daddy," Mike started. "I want to take them off in the family room."

"Now, now," I said, "no complaints. Joy to the world, and all that!"

" 'Cause it's Christmas!" Jenny shrilled, but her voice didn't pierce through me as it had earlier.

"That's right," I said and bent down to help with her boots but kissed her cheek instead.

"You tickle!" she giggled and put her fat little arms around my neck. I bent closer to the boots, so she wouldn't see my eyes. I was feeling very rich.

We had our family time together before the living room fire. I never heard the stranger leave, but then it must have been sometime after the "Alleluia." I can't imagine he would have left before that heavenly "Alleluia."

"THIS HAS BEEN a lovely evening," Sally sighed as she tied the ribbon on the last package. "The nicest Christmas Eve I can remember."

"Yes," I said. "Thanks to you. Everything looks so beautiful and smells so good."

She laughed. "It's the same every year. I didn't think you noticed—except for the bills."

"Well, I noticed, and I like it."

"It was your music that did it for me," she said. "I wouldn't have thought of Mozart for Christmas Eve, but it's perfect. You have no idea how it felt to open the door and hear that magnificent 'Exultate' come pouring out." She smiled. "What a wonderful idea."

Then I remembered the horse and the stranger I'd left in the family room. "Oh, Sally," I said rushing down the hall. "I totally forgot . . ."

I opened the door. He was gone, of course. I think

I was relieved. I'm sure I wouldn't have known how to explain him.

Sally was behind me. "You did it," she exclaimed. "Good work." Then I realized that the horse was no longer sagging but stood upright, proudly stretched on all four legs—ready to gallop its way into Christmas morning. The stranger had kept his side of the bargain.

So here I sit trying to figure it all out. Who would believe that a man who is still closer kin to Scrooge than to Tiny Tim would, on a bleak midwinter night, be visited by an angel?

I think I'll go put on the Mozart.

The Handmaid of the Lord

PEOPLE THINK WHEN your father is the minister that you get special favors, like you were God's pet or something. Rachel, for one, knew absolutely, positively that it was not true. God didn't love her better than Jason McMillan, who was getting an entire set of Mighty Morphin Power Rangers for Christmas. God didn't love her better than that Carrie Wilson, who was getting a new Barbie dollhouse with two new dolls, outfits included. Not that Rachel really wanted a Barbie dollhouse, or Power Rangers either, for that matter, but it was the principle of the thing. Carrie and Jason were getting what they asked Santa Claus for. When Rachel asked Santa for a horse, John and Beth just rolled their eyes. John and Beth were her older brother and sister. Beth was eleven and John, thirteen, and they thought they knew everything.

"But where would we keep a horse, Rachel?" her mother had asked. She was changing baby David's diapers and not paying Rachel much attention. "We live in the church manse. You know how small our yard is."

"Rachel," her father had said in his most patient voice, "what is Christmas really about? If all you think about is Santa Claus, you're going to miss the main event." Rachel's heart sank. When your father told you to think what Christmas was *really* about, she knew what that meant. It meant no horse. Not even a pony. Ministers' kids never got really good presents at Christmas. She should know that by now. It didn't count if you were naughty or nice. Gregory Austin had pulled the alarm last Sunday and made the fire trucks come in the middle of church service, but he was getting his own personal computer. His daddy had said so. Her daddy told everybody they were supposed to be God's servants. Like Jesus was. He didn't even mention presents.

So—no good presents. Rachel had given up on that. But a big role in the primary classes' Christmas play—that shouldn't be too much to ask for. She was by far the best actress in the second grade. *Plus* she went to Sunday school every single week, even when she had the sniffles, or it snowed so hard that she and John and Beth were the only kids there.

"Don't you think a kid who comes every single Sunday no matter if it's a blizzard should get a good part in the primary classes' play?" she asked.

"We live next door to the church, stupid," John had said. "You don't get brownie points for walking across your side yard."

"You're the minister's daughter, Rachel," Beth had said. "It would look bad if you grabbed a big part."

"You got to be Angel Gabriel in both the second *and* third grade," Rachel reminded her.

"That was different," Beth said. "I was the only one in either class who could remember all the lines. The head angel has a lot to say. Besides I speak out. Everyone in the back row heard me perfectly."

"I can speak out," Rachel said, but no one paid any attention.

When she was five, she had been part of the heavenly host. It was a terrible part. The angel costumes were made of a stiff gauzy stuff that itched something awful. Afterward Mrs. MacLaughlin, who ran the pageant, yelled at her right in front of everybody.

"Rachel Thompson! Angels are spiritual beings! They do not scratch themselves while they sing! You had the congregation laughing at the heavenly host. I was mortified."

Last year Mrs. MacLaughlin had taken a rest from directing, and Ms. Westford had run the pageant. Ms. Westford believed in equal opportunity, so for the first time in the history of First Presbyterian Church, girls had been shepherds and wise men. That was okay with the girls, but the boys were mad. They didn't like the itchy angel costumes at all. And a *lot* of the fathers complained.

But Rachel had been a much better shepherd than those stupid boys. She didn't care what anyone had said afterward. She knew what the Bible meant when it said the shepherds were "sore afraid." When Mr. Nelson shined the spotlight at them to show that the angel of the Lord was about to come upon them, Rachel had shown everyone in the church what it meant to be "sore afraid."

"Help! Help!" she'd cried loud enough to be heard by the people in the very back row. "Don't let it get me!"

The congregation laughed. So did Gabriel and all the shepherds and the entire heavenly host. Mary laughed so hard she started choking, and Joseph had to whack her on the back.

Her father said later that it had been "a brand-new insight on the Christmas story," and her mother said, "Never mind, dear, they weren't laughing at you." But she knew better. No one in the whole church understood what the story was really about. When the Bible said "sore afraid," you were supposed to be scared. When that big light hit her face, Rachel had been trembly all over. She knew in her heart that she was the only kid in the pageant who felt that way. Not even the second- and third-graders who got all the big parts did them right. If you couldn't have a scratching angel, you sure shouldn't have a Joseph yawning so wide you could drive a tractor trailer straight down to his tonsils.

It had been a hard year. Her mother had been tired and pregnant for most of it, and then when David finally was born she'd gotten tired and busy. Beth thought David was the "cutest thing in the world."

"Was I cute when I was little?" Rachel asked her.

"I can't remember," Beth said. "I know you cried

a lot. And your face got really red." And she went back to goo-gooing at the baby.

John wasn't as silly, but he was always bragging about how great it was to have a little brother *finally*.

"What's the matter with little sisters?" Rachel asked. John just rolled his eyes.

Now at the end of the worst year of her entire life, Christmas wasn't going to be any better. Even the carols were against her. All those songs about the City of David. "Couldn't we make up a Christmas song about the City of Rachel?" she asked her mother. But her mother just smiled and kept on singing about David.

"Hey," John said one night, "I just realized. We're all in the Christmas story—David, Elizabeth, John—"

"What about me?" Rachel said.

"Oh, you're in it," John said.

"I am?"

"Yeah. I can't remember the verse, but there's something off the side of the story about somebody named Rachel weeping and wailing."

"It's because King Herod killed all her children," Beth said.

It wasn't fair. Everyone else had a nice place in the story—everyone but Rachel. It made her more determined than ever to have a good part in the play, one in which she would not scratch or yell or wail. Mary. She would be Mary. She was old enough this year. She was the best actress in the second grade. Surely, even if she was the minister's daughter, Mrs. MacLaughlin would pick her. She'd be so good in class that Mrs. MacLaughlin would just see that nobody deserved to be Mary more than Rachel did.

Besides, her little brother had already been chosen to be Baby Jesus. She ought to be Mary. Jesus shouldn't have a stranger be his mother. It might scare him.

"Now," said Mrs. MacLaughlin at the first practice. "It's a good thing we have a lot of kindergarten to third-graders in this church because we have a lot of parts in this play."

"Mrs. MacLaughlin?" Rachel said.

"What is it, Rachel?" Mrs. MacLaughlin's voice sounded a tiny bit impatient, so Rachel talked fast.

"I know I'm the minister's kid and that when I was little, sometimes—"

"Yes, Rachel—"

"Well, I've studied the part really hard, and since my brother is the Baby Jesus, I thought, well, it would probably mean a lot to *him* if—well, if his big sister could be Mary."

"But we don't have sixth-graders in the play, Rachel. Elizabeth's too old."

"I don't mean Elizabeth, Mrs. MacLaughlin. I mean, well, what's the matter with me?"

There was a burst of laughter in the room. Everyone was laughing at her! Rachel's face went scarlet. "Shut up!" she yelled. "I'm serious. I know the story better than anybody here, and it's my brother!" Everyone laughed harder. Even the little ones who were going to be itchy angels were giggling.

"Rachel—dear—" said Mrs. MacLaughlin after she finally got control of the group. "Of course you know the Christmas story—after all, your father is our minister—but—but Mary is a very difficult role."

"I could do it," Rachel muttered, but she knew it was no use. People weren't supposed to laugh at Mary. And everybody laughed at her—when they paid her any attention at all.

"Carrie," Mrs. MacLaughlin was saying. "How would you like to be our Mary this year?"

Carrie Wilson? She had blue eyes and blond curls all the way down her back and didn't look at all like Mary. And that fake smile. It made Rachel sick to her stomach. Carrie Wilson's Mary would look like a plastic wimp. Mary was the handmaid of the

Lord, for heaven's sake, not some department-store dummy.

Rachel could hardly listen as Mrs. MacLaughlin went down the list telling everyone what they were supposed to be. She knew now she wouldn't even get a speaking part. Mrs. MacLaughlin didn't like her. Nobody liked her. Not even God. Finally, Mrs. MacLaughlin stopped.

Rachel looked up. She hadn't heard her name. She didn't want to say anything because maybe her name had been called when she wasn't listening and then Mrs. MacLaughlin would have something else to fuss about. But she couldn't stand it. She raised her hand.

"Yes, Rachel?"

"About my part—"

"Yes, Rachel. This year you have a *very* important part."

"I do?"

"Yes. You will be our understudy."

"Our what?"

"Since you know the story *so* well, you will be prepared to *substitute* in case any of our actors become ill or unable to perform."

"Substitute? You mean I don't have a part of my own?"

"You have *all* the parts—in case— Why suppose, for example, Gabriel should lose her voice? You would step in and be our Gabriel."

Jennifer Rouse, the third-grader who had been chosen to be Gabriel, gave Rachel a dirty look. She had no intention of losing her voice. "Or if"—here Mrs. MacLaughlin smiled sadly at Carrie Wilson—"our Mary were to suddenly have to visit her grandmother in Ohio, you would have to step in and be our Mary."

"My grandmother's coming *here* for Christmas, Mrs. MacLaughlin," Carrie said sweetly. Rachel wasn't stupid. She knew what Mrs. MacLaughlin was doing. She wasn't keeping Rachel from having a big part. She was making sure that Rachel wouldn't have any part at all.

SHE TOLD HER MOTHER that she was never going back to Sunday school again in her whole entire life. "Nonsense, dear," her mother said. And, of course, she went back. Ministers' children have to go to Sunday school. It's the law or something.

And then, a miracle happened. One week before Christmas, Carrie Wilson, who wore the world's prissiest little blue leather boots, slipped on the ice in the mall parking lot and broke both her arms. *Both* her arms. Rachel was overcome with exceeding great joy. God did love her. He did! One arm might count as an accident, but two arms were a miracle. God meant business. No matter how determined Mrs. Mac-Laughlin was to keep her out of the play, God was going to make sure not only that she got in but that she got the most important part in the whole shebang. She was going to be Mary, the handmaid of the Lord.

Of course, she didn't tell anybody how joyful she was. She was too smart for that. When Mrs. Mac-Laughlin called her on the phone, Rachel practically cried at the news that she would have to pinch-hit for our poor little Carrie. "I'll do my best, Mrs. Mac-Laughlin," she said quietly and humbly, just like the real Mary would have.

She went early to the dress rehearsal so Mrs. MacLaughlin could try the costume on her. It fit perfectly. Well, it would have fit practically anybody. Those robe things weren't exactly any size, but Rachel took it as a good sign when Mrs. MacLaughlin sighed and admitted that, yes, it did fit.

"Don't you worry, Mrs. MacLaughlin," Rachel said. "I'm the understudy. I know the part perfectly." Which was a little silly since Mary didn't say a word, just looked lovingly into the manger while everyone else sang and carried on. But she wanted Mrs. Mac-Laughlin to know she wasn't going to do anything to make anybody laugh this year. She would be such a good Mary that Mrs. MacLaughlin would be practically down on her knees begging her to take the part again next year. They'd probably have to extend the play past third grade so that they could keep Rachel in the role of Mary until she was grown up and through college and had babies of her own.

"We have to eat early," she told her mother on Christmas Eve. "Mrs. MacLaughlin wants the cast there an hour before the service."

"Thank goodness," said John. "I don't think I could stand another hour of loud glorias sung off-key."

But Rachel didn't care. She was so happy, the glorias just burst from her. Besides, she had to get them all out before seven o'clock. She couldn't let a stray gloria pass her lips when she was behind that manger. God might understand, but Mrs. MacLaughlin sure wouldn't.

She was all dressed in the sky-blue robe, sitting quietly, looking down into the empty manger. Mrs. MacLaughlin, hoarse from yelling at the heavenly hosts, was giving last-minute directions to the wise men, when suddenly the back door of the sanctuary opened.

"Why, Mrs. Wilson. Carrie——" Mrs. MacLaughlin said.

Rachel jerked up in alarm. It *was* Carrie, standing in the darkened sanctuary, her fake-fur-trimmed coat hanging off her shoulders, both arms bound to the front of her body.

"She insisted," Mrs. Wilson was saying. "She said, 'The show must go on.' I talked to Dr. Franklin, and he said it would be the best thing in the world for her. She was so distressed about letting everyone down that it was having a negative effect on the healing process——"

Two mothers yanked the beautiful blue robe off Rachel and draped it over Carrie's head. "See. It was meant to be," Mrs. Wilson said. "It totally hides the casts."

Rachel slunk off the platform and slumped down in the first pew. No one noticed. All the adults were oohing and ahing about how brave Carrie was to come and save the play.

"Oh, yes, she's in terrible pain," her mother was saying. "But she couldn't bear to disappoint you all."

No one cared that Rachel was disappointed. Not even God. Of course, God had known all along that

Carrie would show up at the last minute and steal back the part. God knew everything, and he had let Rachel sing and rejoice and think for a few days that he was on her side, that he had chosen her, like Mary, to be his handmaid. But it was just a big joke. A big, mean joke. She kicked the red carpet at her feet.

"Off stage, off stage, everyone. Time to line up in your places."

Where did you go when there wasn't any place for you? She looked around. People were beginning to arrive for the service. She slipped farther down in the pew. She didn't want her family to see her. They'd find out soon enough that God had fired her.

She saw her mother carry David up the far aisle. The baby was sucking happily on his pacifier. He would be a good Jesus. Everyone would say so. Mrs. MacLaughlin was waiting at the door to the hall. She took David and said something to Mom, who cocked her head in a doubtful manner. Was she telling Mom that Rachel wasn't going to be Mary after all? If she did, maybe Mom would come over and take her on her lap and tell her she was sorry. No, Mom didn't even look her way.

The play went well. None of the angels cried or scratched. Gabriel knew all her lines and said them loud enough to be heard almost to the back row. The wise men remembered to carry in their gifts and nobody's crown rolled off. Joseph did not yawn, and Mary gazed sweetly into the manger. It was all perfect. Perfect without her. Rachel felt like weeping and wailing like the Rachel in the Bible.

And then, suddenly, a miracle occurred. Baby Jesus began to cry. Not just cry, *scream*. Yell his little lungs out. Carrie Wilson forgot about being Mary. She turned absolutely white, and her eyes went huge, like she was about to panic. She would have probably got up and run, but with her arms bound under her robe she couldn't move. She looked at Joseph. "Do something!" she whispered. Joseph's face went bright red, but he didn't move a muscle.

It was all up to Rachel. She jumped from her pew and dashed up the chancel steps. She was still panting when she got to the manger. Rachel poked around under the baby until she located the pacifier and jammed it into David's open mouth. He clamped down on it at once. The big church went silent except for his noisy sucking. Rachel smiled down at him. He was a lovely Jesus.

"Who do you think you are?" Carrie Wilson hissed through her teeth. But the whisper was almost loud enough to be heard in the back row. Rachel could hear a snicker from somewhere out in the darkened sanctuary.

"Behold." Rachel straightened up and stared sternly in the direction of the offender. There was no doubt that the people in the last pew could hear her. "I am the handmaid of the Lord! And I say unto you, glory to God in the highest and on earth peace and goodwill to men, women, and children."

Nobody laughed. They didn't dare.

My Name Is Joseph

In the sixth month the angel Gabriel was sent from God to a city of Galilee named Nazareth, to a virgin betrothed to a man whose name was Joseph, of the house of David; and the virgin's name was Mary.

MY NAME IS Joseph. In Spanish I am called José. But I have not always spoken Spanish. I learned it from the old priest who came to our mountain village when I was a boy. My people are Indians, descendants of the great Maya. Our civilization is older than the Christian era. The priest said I should be very proud, but it is hard to be proud when your belly is empty.

Before I was born our people owned rich farm-lands, but a *yanqui* company needed those lands for coffee, and since we were only Indians, the government moved us deeper into the mountains to land no one else wanted.

My parents were dead, so the priest became a father to me. He taught me to read and write, and the year after his coming, at the Feast of the Annunciation, he baptized me. It was he who named me José. He told me that just as Joseph was given the care of the infant Jesus, so I must always care for those weaker than myself.

When I was a boy, I obeyed him and helped him, but as a young man I became rebellious. It was hard enough to get food for myself—how could I worry about others? I know it must have saddened the heart of my foster father to see me go down to the coffee plantations at harvesttime to make a little money and then waste it on drink and women in the town. Seven years ago, I returned to the village after the harvest to find that the old priest had died.

At first I was pleased. I am ashamed to say it now, but with him gone there was no one to look sad and shake his head at my behavior. And besides, he had left his house to me. It was not large, but it was all mine.

It only took a few days to discover the rest of my inheritance. He had left me the entire village. Everyone who was sick or hungry or afraid would come to my door.

"Go away!" I said to them. "I am not a priest. The priest is dead."

"You can read," an old woman said to me. "The father taught you. You must be our priest now. We have no other."

Little by little, whether it was my own guilt or the Spirit of God, I became the leader of my village. I did not perform the Mass, of course, but they pleaded with me until I read the sacred words to them each week. At night, after the day's work was done, those who wanted to learn would gather in my little house, and I would try to teach them to read from the old priest's Spanish Bible. Since most of them did not speak Spanish, only the Indian dialect of our village, this was a discouraging task. But they were grateful and gave me gifts of maize or beans that they would not allow me to refuse.

My wife, Elena Maria, was one of my pupils. She was a clever, bright-eyed young girl, who learned quickly and soon began to help me with the others.

We were married and in three years had two sons and a third child on the way.

I have not mentioned the political situation in my country. Our village was quite remote, you see. The soil was poor, and there was no true road. We were many days' walk from the nearest coffee plantation, and at least five miles from another Indian village. It had been a long time since anyone in our village had had enough surplus to make the long journey to market.

I, who used to go farther down the mountain to work, no longer left the village. There was too much to do. We had begun to work together. We shared seed and combined our tiny plots into larger fields to grow our beans and maize more efficiently and to let some of the land rest and recover its strength. A farmer I had met some years before in the town had told me this secret.

I was hoeing maize in the large village field the day I saw guerrillas coming up the side of the mountain. I did not know at first that they were guerrillas. I could see only a band of Indians—say twenty-five or so—climbing up toward us. As the leader of my village, I went down to meet them, followed by my people. Then I saw the old rifles slung over their shoulders and the machetes hung at their belts. There were both men and women; some were almost children; four or five were old enough to be fathers to me.

"Why do you come with guns?" I asked. I had to sound very brave because my people were standing just behind me.

"We do not come to harm you, my brother." The leader of the band was a man my own age. "We come to warn you. The soldiers are searching the mountain villages for communists."

"We have nothing to fear," I said. "There are no communists among us." I was, in fact, the only one in the village who knew what the word *communist* meant.

"Who is your leader?"

"You are speaking to him," I said.

"Are you a catechist?" the man asked.

"I teach my people what I know," I answered. "We have no priest."

"Your children look better fed than most."

"It is because we help each other in this village," I said, not without a little pride.

"You teach people to read and write, and you co-operate in your farming?"

"Yes," I said. His question seemed foolish to me.

"For this, my brother," he said softly, "they will

call you a communist, and they will kill you. You had better join us."

But I did not go with them. I was Joseph, given the care of the weak and the young. I had no stomach for rifles and fighting. Besides, I did not know these people. They might well be lying.

A WEEK LATER a single stranger made her way up the mountain. She was from a village fifty miles to the south and west of us. She asked which direction the guerrillas had gone. Elena, seeing how tired and hungry the visitor was, took her to our house and gave her food. The woman gave us her story. The soldiers had come to her village and demanded to know where the communists were being hidden.

"We knew no communists," the woman said. "We had heard rumors of a guerrilla band in the mountains behind us, but none of us had seen them. The soldiers refused to believe us. They took our five strongest men away in their truck. Next day, we found their mutilated bodies in the road." She stopped speaking for a moment. We waited in silence. "One of them," she said, "was my husband.

"The soldiers came again. 'See how cruel the communists are,' they said. 'We questioned your men and let them go. Now those villains have slaughtered them—' " She stopped again, fixing her eyes on my two-year-old son resting in his mother's lap. "I was crazy with grief, so I shouted, 'You lie! You did this crime yourselves!' They killed my children before my eyes with their machetes. Then they raped me and left me for dead." Her eyes flashed with hatred. "I go now to join the rebellion in the mountains. Tell me where they are!"

We could not tell her, but the following day she went on, leaving dread behind her like dense fog on the mountain.

We had one more warning. Another woman, from the village nearest to our own, told me that if I did not leave, the whole village would suffer. But how could I flee alone without my sons and Elena? We left togther, taking almost nothing, because we knew the children would tire quickly and we would have to carry them.

And Joseph also went up from Galilee, from the city of Nazareth, to Judea, to the city of David, which is called Bethlehem, because he was of the house and lineage of David, to be enrolled with Mary, his betrothed, who was with child.

I thought of Joseph, my namesake, as we crossed the mountains, traveling north in the cold mists of darkness. We were afraid to travel by day. When light came, we would lie crouched under the cover of foliage, sometimes sleeping, sometimes listening to a helicopter searching the mountainsides for signs of those in hiding there. I have heard of the black slaves of your own country, who followed the North Star to freedom. In the Scriptures, it is the wise men who follow the star, but I did not feel very wise. I, Joseph, whose wife was great with child, was searching, not for the land of my forefathers but for someplace, anyplace where my child might be born in safety.

We ran out of food within three days. We had tried to be careful, but the children were hungry, and we could not let them cry. Someone might hear.

God sent angels to watch over us. One was an old man hunting birds. We came upon his solitary fire one night, too hungry for proper caution.

"Ah, my children," he said, "my little children, God did not mean for you to suffer so." And he fed us roasted dove and beans wrapped in tortillas, and we shared his cup of boiled coffee. It was the first time I had seen the little boys smile since we left our village.

"There are some of our people in hiding two days'

walk from here," he told us. "They will help you get into Mexico." Our angel gave us beans and tortillas and a little meat for our journey.

We walked for three nights, seeing no one, but at dawn on the third day, the lookout for the guerrilla camp found us and led us to his compatriots. I did not know these people. It was a different band from those who had come through our village. The leader was a young woman. She asked my name. When I told her, she said, "I have heard this name. They are searching for you." Her words chilled me because I knew that my people had suffered because of me. And that was true. Many had died. Our pigs and goats and foodstuffs had been stolen. The village was burned.

I should have stayed, I thought, I should have died for them. But how could I have stayed and caused my wife and sons to die as well? I am not God that I can weigh one life against another. Surely, as the hunter said, God did not mean for any of us to suffer so. What harm have we done that we should be punished? We only ask to be left alone to live out our humble lives as God wills, to bring our children into the world without fear. We did not dream of riches or power—only that our little ones might lie down at night without the pain of an empty stomach.

"Why don't you join us?" the young woman said, seeing how I grieved for my village.

But I could not. Perhaps it was only selfishness, perhaps distaste for killing, but I wanted to take my sons and my wife and my child not yet acquainted with the sorrows of this world—I wanted to take them to a place of peace. Then if I died, it would not matter. They would know that I had been Joseph to them.

"I cannot help you now," I said to the leader, "but if you help me, perhaps someday God will let me repay you." She was not happy to hear my decision, but there were already many children to care for in their camp, so the guerrillas gave us food and directions to a convent just over the border.

"They will feed you there," she said, "and find you a place to live."

I thought once we crossed into Mexico we would be safe. I cannot tell you how light my heart was the night we came to the convent. It was the Feast Day of Saint Nicholas, and as we celebrated our first Mass in many years, I rejoiced. Saint Nicholas had loved the poor. Surely, he would aid us. After Mass, the sisters fed us a warm meal of red beans and rice. They gave us hot water to bathe with and clean cots to sleep upon. We felt we had reached heaven itself.

The next day we learned differently. We could not live in that village. Soldiers had come just two nights before. They had followed refugees across the border, dragged them from the houses where they had sought to hide, put them in trucks, and headed south. Their bodies had been left along the border as a warning both to those who might wish to flee and to those tempted to take them in. There were "ears" in the village, the sisters told me, informers who told our soldiers when strangers came to the village. And the Mexican police could not, or would not, protect fugitives.

"Elena and I speak Spanish," I said. "We will pretend to be Mexican Indians."

"Your children will betray you," the Reverend Mother said sadly. "They are too young. They will forget and speak their own dialect." I knew she was right.

The sisters gave us a huge basket of food, a little money, and tickets for buses going north. They took away our beautiful woven Indian garments and dressed us as poor Mexicans. Last of all they gave Elena a large bag of sweets. "You must keep the children's mouths full of candy," the Reverend Mother said, "so they will not speak."

And while they were there, the time came for her to be delivered. And she gave birth to her firstborn son and wrapped him in swaddling cloths, and laid him in a manger, because there was no place for them in the inn.

On that long trip from La Trinitaria to Nuevo Laredo, I thought often of the child that Elena carried. My first hope, of course, was that he would not choose to be born on a bus—that he would wait until we reached the safety of the Benedictine community that had promised to care for us. In our village, birthing is women's work; I did not want Elena to have to count on me when her hour came. And if we had to stop, had to ask for help, how long could we keep our nationality secret?

But God is good. When Mexican police boarded the bus we rode, Elena and I pretended to sleep and prayed that the wide-eyed boys, their mouths bulging with sweets, would not speak. How many times did we change from one crowded, dirty bus to another? I cannot remember. I only remember the young man who came up to me when we got off the last bus in Nuevo Laredo. He spoke my name softly. When I nodded, he said, "Follow me."

At the community they greeted us with great kindness. "Poor little mother," they said of Elena. "We must get her across the Rio Grande as soon as possible. The children you can keep quiet, but an infant—"

How could I ask her to travel farther? I looked at my once beautiful young wife, her body sagging with the weight of the child and her own exhaustion. Did they know how many nights she had walked, how many days and nights she had ridden? "Let us stay until after the New Year," I begged. "In January, when the child is still tiny and will hardly make a sound . . ."

But it was Elena who persuaded me. "If the child is born in the United States," she argued, "he is a citizen. They cannot send a citizen to an alien land to die. A citizen has many rights. The sister told me."

And so it was arranged. An American priest was coming with a young man, his nephew. They would be driving a van. In the back of the van, the young man had built a bed. They would take out the side of the bed, and we would climb under it and be nailed in. Tiny holes had been drilled close to the mattress so that we would have air to breathe. I was terrified by such a plan. Suppose, despite the candy, one of the boys should cry out in fright? Suppose Elena's time came?

Suppose the border guards discovered us and sent us back to our homeland?

I saw the young man and his uncle the priest just minutes before I helped my family into our hiding place and crawled in behind them. The youth was chewing gum and wearing American cowboy boots. A most unlikely angel, I thought. But the Reverend Mother introduced him to me. "This is Christopher," she said. I remembered the joy I had felt on Saint Nicholas's Day. God was sending me still another sign—Christopher, the Christ bearer, the saint who carried the infant Jesus to safety when Herod pursued the Holy Family. He would deliver us from harm.

It may seem like blasphemy to you, but as I lay there in the darkness, aware of each shallow breath from the bodies of my dear ones pressed so closely against my own, feeling the movement of the child in Elena's womb, my heart went out to this one yet unborn. It was not the firstborn—it was not even perhaps a son—and I was not a righteous man, but somehow that innocent life was Jesus to me. I, Joseph, hiding in the dark, was powerless, but surely God must protect his own.

I could hear the muffled voices of our benefactors.

I knew when they stopped and paid the bridge toll. I could tell from the growl of many engines and the choking smell of petrol that the bridge was crowded with holiday traffic. We must not cough, no matter how noxious the fumes. The van moved forward so slowly, so terribly slowly. Elena shifted against me. I realized that she was stroking the boys, hoping they would sleep.

At last we came to the border. I heard a strange North American voice—the police. He was asking questions at the window. The priest and Christopher got out. My heart stopped beating. "Holy God, holy God," I said to myself over and over, the only prayer I could manage. Someone opened the back doors of the van. I waited for the jolt that would tell me the policeman had boarded and would begin his search. I did not dare even to reach my hand to my wife or to try to cover my younger son's mouth. I lay there frozen, waiting.

The doors banged shut. The van shuddered. No one had climbed aboard. The front doors opened and then closed. I heard English words even I could understand. "Okay, father. Merry Christmas to you." The van moved forward, slowly at first, and then gradually up to a normal speed. Beside me I could feel Elena's body heave with sobs she still did not dare let loose. I, too, was crying.

OUR DAUGHTER WAS born later that same night, not in a stable—in the back of a 1978 Plymouth van, thirty miles south of San Antonio, Texas. In the end it was I who held out my hands and welcomed her tiny wet body into this world. Neither the priest, nor the one called Christopher, dared to perform this simple office. I laughed; how easy, how joyful it was to greet this infant. I was singing with the angels, "Gloria, gloria, gloria."

I wrapped her in a blanket the nuns had given me and held her for her brothers and her rescuers to see. "Her name is Esperanza," I said.

"*Esperanza* means hope," the priest explained to young Christopher.

"Hope." I tried this new English word in my mouth. It tasted sweeter than the children's candy. I looked up at the bright stars—the same ones shining down on the mountains of my ruined village.

"Someday," I said to the infant in my arms, "someday peace will come to our mountains, and I will take you there. Hope will come to my people."

Until then, with the help of God and His saints, and all the holy angels, I will watch over this blessed child.

My name is Joseph.

About the Author

Katherine Paterson was born in China, the daughter of missionary parents. Educated in both China and the United States, she graduated from King College in Bristol, Tennessee, and received a master's degree from the Presbyterian School of Christian Education in Richmond, Virginia. After studying and working in Japan for four years, she was awarded a fellowship to Union Theological Seminary in New York City, where she met her husband, the Reverend John B. Paterson. The Patersons have four grown children and two grandchildren and live in Barre, Vermont.

A two-time recipient of both the Newbery Medal and National Book Award for her novels, Katherine

Paterson has also published essays and written a book in collaboration with her husband. A previous collection of Christmas stories, *Angels and Other Strangers*, was published by Crowell (now HarperCollins) in 1979.